Brides of ~~~~~~~

by Cat Cahill

All rights reserved. No part of this publication may be reproduced, distributed, or transmitted in any form or by any means, including photocopying, recording, or other electronic or mechanical methods, without the prior written permission of the author, except in the case of brief quotations embodied in critical reviews and certain other noncommercial uses permitted by copyright law. For permission requests, write to the author at:

http://www.catcahill.com[1]

This is a work of fiction. Names, characters, businesses, places, events, locales, and incidents are either the products of the author's imagination or used in a fictitious manner. Any resemblance to actual persons, living or dead, or actual events is purely coincidental.

Copyright © 2020 as Dejected in Denver, Cat Cahill
Copyright © 2021 as Molly, Cat Cahill
Cover design by Black Widow Books
All rights reserved.

---

1. http://www.catcahill.com/

Chapter One

CAÑON CITY, COLORADO - Spring 1881

Molly Hill narrowed her eyes at her sister-in-law as Grace returned to her small dress shop in the rear of the family's general store. Grace didn't notice. She was too busy smiling at nothing and placing a hand against her stomach. Grace had a secret, and Molly was almost certain she knew what it was.

Grace was expecting a baby.

Molly would have to ask her about it later, after she figured out whether Jasper knew yet. Her brother was hardly perceptive about such things. As Grace disappeared into the dress shop, Molly glanced about the general store and sighed. There were no customers right now. She wished for someone—anyone—to walk in. She much preferred helping customers to tallying the receipts that were laid out in front of her.

As if it read her mind, the door opened and a tall man with a worn brown hat and a star-shaped badge pinned to his coat strode inside.

Deputy Eli Jennings.

He fixed her with that smile she'd come to know so well, the one that made his eyes crinkle just so and made her wonder how he didn't have every girl in town falling at his feet. For a brief time last summer, when he'd been charged with escorting Molly and her mother safely to and from the store each day, she thought he might have taken a shine to her. But nothing had ever come of it, and so she'd figured he saw her as a sister—just like every other eligible man in town. Molly Hill, little sister to every marriageable man in Fremont County.

Molly sighed again and fixed a smile on her face for Eli.

"Afternoon, Miss Molly," he said as he removed his hat.

"Hello, Eli." She tried to sound cheerful, but lately the fear she might never marry had begun to consume her. It had started out small, sometime after Jasper had married Grace, and then had grown bit by bit until it seemed she thought of it each time she so much as saw a happy couple or one of the young men she'd known for years.

His brilliant smile faded into a look of concern. "Are you well?"

"I'm fine." Molly forced the lonely feelings down. It was hardly Eli's fault, and he looked genuinely concerned for her. If she concentrated on the here and now, the feelings wouldn't trouble her. "Are you here to see Jasper?" She already knew the answer—Eli arrived daily to talk briefly with her brother. After the danger they'd found themselves in last summer with the attempted prison break, Eli had made it his appointed duty to stop by each afternoon. It was unnecessary, but the man took his work as a sheriff's deputy seriously, and for that, Molly admired him.

He was also quite handsome, with thick, light brown hair, hazel eyes, and of course, that smile that lit up a room. But she would never tell him that. He might get a big head, and besides, thinking about such things only made her start to feel down about her situation again.

"Is he in the storeroom?" Eli asked, his eyes drifting toward the room's closed door.

"He is." Molly began stacking the receipts as she spoke. She didn't have the mind for them at this moment, anyway.

Eli turned that smile toward her again, and it only made her want to smile too. What must it be like to walk about like Eli, who appeared to have no concerns in the world?

"I've brought you the paper." He set a freshly printed *Fremont County Record* on the counter where her receipts had been. "I know how much you look forward to it each week," he explained as if he didn't already bring her the paper every Saturday.

Molly laid a hand on the paper, eager to see how this week's advertisement for Hill's General Store and Dress Shop.

"I haven't read it yet, but that news about Billy the Kid looks mighty interesting." Eli nodded at the paper.

Molly glanced down to have some clue about the story of which he spoke. "Yes, it does. I'll be certain to read it." She enjoyed learning about the latest news and worldly events, even if she'd begun looking at the newspaper for their weekly advertisment.

"I'll purchase another copy for myself, and perhaps we can discuss it at some point." Eli smiled at her again, and Molly's heart tripped a little faster. It was a strange sort of thing for him to say, and she didn't know why it made her feel so nervous.

He wants an intelligent conversation, that's all, she told herself as Eli nodded at her before moving toward the storeroom to find her brother.

Molly glanced about the store. She knew her mother was in the dress shop at the rear with Grace and the two men were in the storeroom. She drew in a breath, enjoying a rare moment alone.

She opened the paper and flipped past articles about Washington, DC and the state government in Denver, news about who was new in town and who'd left Cañon City. And there it was. She grinned at the large advertisement Jasper had purchased and for which Molly had created the wording. It declared Hill's General Store and Dress Shop had numerous goods in stock and the finest dressmaker in town. That last claim ought to make horrible Harold Trace, the only other dressmaker in Cañon City, red with fury.

She closed the paper, setting it aside to read more thoroughly later, and forcing herself to look at the stack of receipts again. Jasper and Eli's voices drifted in from the storeroom, along with Grace's laughter from the little dress shop in back. Molly sighed. Everyone seemed contented with their lot in life—except for her.

And yet, most who knew her would think otherwise. She'd grown up here in Cañon City, and knew most folks who walked in their doors. But here she was, twenty-four years old and with no prospects for marriage.

It seemed impossible sometimes, when Molly thought hard on it, and yet there it was. Not a one of the men she knew thought of her as a woman to court and marry. She was Molly, the girl who worked with her brother at the general store and who climbed trees with them when they were young. Cañon City saw its share of new men to town, but yet each time she thought she'd caught the eye of one of them, he became only a friend.

So instead of a life filled with knowing glances and the anticipation of starting a family, like Jasper and Grace had, Molly was teetering on the edge of spinsterhood.

She flipped through the receipts without really looking at them. It did no good to feel sorry for herself, but it was hard not to when it seemed her life had one, very much unwanted path for her to follow. It reminded her of a young man who'd come into the store earlier today. He'd purchased a small amount of equipment and other necessities to ride south, into the mountains, to join up with a silver mining operation. He was a sad-looking sort of a fellow, perhaps only a few years younger than she. He'd told her that the girl he'd planned to marry in Denver had recently passed from a fever. Not knowing what else to do, he'd left Denver to start life anew elsewhere.

Jasper always said she knew more about their customers than the customers knew about themselves, but Molly truly enjoyed striking up conversations with them. They were all so interesting and had such stories to tell. But this man, the one who'd lost the love of his life, had stuck with her today, and it came to mind again as she picked up a pencil to tally the receipts.

He'd left Denver to find a new life south of Cañon City. What must that be like? It was hard to imagine, but now that it had come to her mind, it was also hard for Molly to forget.

Could she do the same?

It was a terrifying and exciting thought. In a place like Denver, which had far more people than Cañon City, she could meet untold numbers of eligible gentlemen. And best of all, none of them would see her as Jasper's little sister, the girl who bested them in a footrace fifteen years ago and who now sold them flour and little trinkets for their sweethearts at the general store. In another place, she could be someone entirely different.

The possibilities danced through her mind, and as she fell asleep that night, one question lingered.

Could she make it happen?

Chapter Two

"WHERE'VE YOU BEEN?" Harry Caldwell, the other regular sheriff's deputy, greeted Eli the second he pushed through the door into the office.

"Out walking the town, no different from usual." Eli paused in his defense to take in Caldwell's cheerful countenance. The older man's hat was off and he was leaning back comfortably in one of the chairs that sat around the desk. Behind the desk, Sheriff Ben Young smirked as he propped his boots up against the nicked wood. Eli thought of these men as family, and he imagined they felt the same, given how they teased him like a little brother.

"And how's Miss Hill?" Young asked, lacing his hands behind his head.

Eli busied himself with pulling off his coat. "She's fine. Why don't you ever ask how her mother is, or the folks over at the McClure?"

"'Cause you ain't sweet on her mother or the folks at the hotel." Caldwell grinned at him. "When are you going to finally ask to court that poor girl?"

Eli didn't answer—because he didn't have an answer. Instead, he strode to the stove in the corner and squatted to add more wood to fight the spring chill that lingered in the air.

"She's not going to wait forever, a pretty girl like that," Young said. "If you want, I can ask Penny—"

"No!" Eli whipped around so hard he slammed his shoulder into the door of the stove. Rubbing the aching spot, he stood and looked his friend right in the eye. "Don't say a word to Mrs. Young."

That made Caldwell start to cackle, and it wasn't long before Young joined in. The sheriff's wife was nothing but kind to Eli, but she took far more interest than she should in his—and everyone else's—romantic life. She'd offered more than once to find him a wife, either in town or through the mail-order bride business she ran with another lady down in Crest Stone.

"I ought to get home to the missus," Caldwell said, rising from his seat after finally sobering from his laugh at Eli's expense. "You want to come for dinner?"

Eli shook his head and thanked him. While Mrs. Caldwell's cooking couldn't be beat, he found himself wanting to be alone.

"All quiet out there?" Young asked after Caldwell left.

"Quiet enough," Eli replied.

"I got word about rustlers a little ways north. I'll ride out in the morning and see what I find." Young stacked a few stray papers as he spoke.

Eli nodded. "I can close up if you want to head upstairs."

"I'll take you up on that. It's been a long day." Young stood and stretched before collecting his hat and coat. "Penny will send down food for the Robbins brothers." The brothers were currently occupying the jail cells behind the office after stealing the payroll off the train bound for the silver mines in the mountains. Considering the sheriff and his wife lived just upstairs of the office, it was more economical for Mrs. Young to simply cook extra and send it down for the prisoners than it was to order food for them from one of the restaurants in town.

"Won't be long before the judge sends them down the road," Eli said, referring to the state penitentiary at the edge of town.

"Sure ought to." Young paused, his coat slung over his shoulder. "Almost forgot—there's a letter for you from Denver. It's in the desk."

Eli bid Young good evening before moving toward the desk. Denver. That had to mean his mother. He knew no one else in the city these days, even though he'd spent nearly all of his younger life there. He found the letter, sliced it open with a knife, and sat back to read.

Dearest Eli,

I hope this letter finds you well, my son. It is cold here in Denver, and I wish I had the company of my family to keep me warm.

Eli paused and breathed out in frustration. While he loved his mother, she was relentless in her attempts to persuade him to return to Denver for good. Being her unmarried son, he was the one who received the bulk of her guilt-inducing attempts, although he was certain his married sisters weren't immune. He sat up and pressed the letter to the desk.

I've found myself in a bit of a pinch lately. You see, Mr. Wenzel finally succeeded in selling your father's company—for a handsome price, I might add—but I've recently discovered my dear Theodore had taken out many debts. They must be repaid, and I fear it will take all I've got left to satisfy the man he owed. I've put the man off by offering him small sums, but I do hope you might write to him and ask if there is some other way.

When you reply, please let me know if you were successful. Also, if you don't have a sweetheart in Cañon City, I've recently met the daughter of a Mrs. Graves. She's quite a bit older than you and she isn't very intelligent, but I believe she'd make a fine wife.

Your loving mother

Eli huffed again and shoved the letter back into its envelope. Wouldn't anyone leave him be with the marriage talk? Between his friends and his mother, one might think Eli was on the verge of living alone on the side of a mountain with a beard clear down to his knees and a herd of mule deer for company.

He set about gathering his things, his ma's letter on his mind. His father had never been indebted in his life, of that Eli was absolutely certain. Theodore Jennings had an impeccable reputation, both in business and in his personal life. He hadn't been rich, by any means, but he'd built up a decent lumberyard and had many friends. It would've broken his heart to know that his only son hadn't returned to take over his business. Eli tried not to think about that too often.

One thing was clear from that letter, though. Ma was in some sort of trouble, and Eli doubted it was something he could solve by simply writing a letter. He'd need to go to Denver, speak to the man in person, and find out what he thought Eli's father owed him. It had to be a misunderstanding. If it wasn't, then either Pa wasn't the man Eli and everyone else had thought he was—which was impossible—or someone was stealing from his mother.

It had been some time since he'd been to Denver, and he owed Ma a visit anyway. He'd be gone a week, at most, he figured as he climbed the stairs to Young's place to get leave to make the journey.

One week, and then he'd be back to the work here that he loved. And a certain woman he wished he could muster up the courage to do more than give a newspaper and make small talk with. He'd never understand how he could face down armed outlaws and not have the guts to be forthright with Molly.

Somehow a pretty face was far more intimidating than a surly man with a pistol.

Chapter Three

MOLLY ARRANGED HER traveling skirt as best she could on the upholstered train seat. She'd chosen a place by the window, and could hardly contain her excitement at making the journey to Denver. She'd never traveled by train before. In fact, she'd never traveled anywhere she could remember. She'd been so young when her family arrived in Cañon City, and she'd never had cause to leave.

But now she was. Her aunt and uncle's home in Denver awaited her, along with the possibility of finding love. When she'd proposed the idea of visiting Aunt Ellen and Uncle John for a few months, Mama had immediately agreed it would be a nice change for her. And when Mama had hinted not-so-subtly that she might find a good man to marry, Molly knew they were of the same mind. Mama had immediately telegraphed her brother and sister-in-law, and now, a few days later, Molly found herself on this train.

She set her beaded reticule in her lap. It was new—a gift from Mama for her trip, as was the hat she wore and, packed away in her trunk, a beautiful new evening dress Grace had made up for a woman in town who'd changed her mind. A few alterations later, and now it fit Molly perfectly. She was all set for her adventure. For meeting new people and most especially, for finding a suitor. Perhaps she'd find two—wouldn't that be the most incredible thing? She could just imagine herself needing to fight off the affections of two handsome, well-to-do, respectable men who'd fallen madly in love with her. The image brought a giggle to her lips and she covered her mouth just before it escaped.

"Pardon me, miss. Might I take this seat?" a male voice asked.

A very familiar male voice.

"Deputy Jennings?" Molly couldn't contain her surprise. Whatever was he doing on this train?

Eli winced a bit at her formality, and Molly traded her shock for a smile.

"What a pleasant surprise to see a familiar face. Please, do sit." She gestured at the seat across from her.

Appeased, he lowered himself onto the cushioned seat, setting a small case next to him. "Are you traveling alone?"

Molly nodded. It was something she and her mother had discussed thoroughly. Mama had worried, but Molly had argued that women made journeys on the train by themselves all the time now. Why, it was almost fashionable to go alone! "I'm going to visit with my aunt and uncle for the summer." She paused as she studied Eli, wondering if she should have told him she was leaving. "I'd noticed you hadn't been by the store in a few days. Does your travel have something to do with the reason you were away?"

Eli removed his hat and set it on top of his case before running a hand through his hair. It made him look nervous. "It did, but only because I had some work to finish up before leaving. I'm going to visit my mother."

"How wonderful! I had a feeling you were a good son."

Eli's face tinged red. "I don't know about that so much, but it's been some time since I've seen her."

"And your father?" She hoped she wasn't being too nosy. It felt as if she was funneling all of her anxiety about the journey into this conversation with Eli. It was something of a relief to have someone she knew on this train with her.

"He passed on, about a year ago. That was the last I've been to Denver." His eyes, which she'd noticed before tended to turn either brown or green depending upon the light, were more of a soft brown shade now with a sad sort of faraway look to them.

"I'm so sorry," Molly said. "I didn't mean to pry." She knew how hard it was to lose a father—her own had passed several years prior. She needed to rein in her nerves before she began asking him about childhood misdeeds, or worse, past sweethearts.

"It's quite all right. I—"

The screech of the train whistle interrupted Eli's words, though it was muffled some from within the carriage with the windows closed. The car lurched forward, and Molly gripped the edge of her seat in one hand, excitement finally overtaking her anxiety. "We're moving," she said, unable to keep the glee from her voice.

She couldn't draw her eyes from the window as the depot passed slowly by, followed by the rest of the town until they were traveling through scrubby brown hills, dotted here and there with silver-green sage and brighter green clumps of spring grasses. The rushing Arkansas River came and went from view as the train journeyed east toward Pueblo.

"It's wonderful, isn't it?" Molly's words were breathless as the land flattened out. They passed a ranch, the buildings off in the distance while cattle stood nearer the train, seemingly unfazed by its motion or noise.

When Eli didn't answer, she drew her attention away from the window to his amused face.

"I take it this is your first experience traveling by train?" he asked.

"It is," Molly admitted. "To be honest, I've never left Cañon City—to my memory, that is. Oh, look!" They were passing another ranch, this one much closer to the tracks, and two little boys waved from where they played in front of a house. Molly waved back, unable to contain her joy at the entire experience. "Aren't they sweet?" She glanced again at Eli, his smile even broader this time. "I'm sorry, you must think me quite silly."

"Not at all. Your enthusiasm is adorable."

She could almost insist she saw a twinkle in his eye when he spoke, and a heavy dose of embarrassment made her go warm from head to toe. "Adorable? You make it sound as if I'm a child or a fluffy kitten."

"You're hardly either," he said. His gaze rested on her face just a moment too long, and Molly shifted, occupying herself with placing her reticule on the seat beside her. Those were exactly the sort of looks he gave her now and then last summer, when he walked Molly and her mother to and from the store. She'd thought for a brief while he'd held some interest in her. She wouldn't have minded if he did. Eli was awfully handsome, with that thick hair and his tall stature. And yet, he'd never breathed a word to match those looks he'd given her—either then or in the months following when she'd catch him watching her just so every now and then. So she'd brushed it off as a misunderstanding on her part. And yet, here he was now, gazing at her with that same expression and making her heart beat a little faster.

Molly didn't know what to make of it, and she soon found her eyes wandering back to the window and the sights to be seen on the other side of it. All sorts of possibilities wound their way through her mind. "Do you suppose we might be held up?" She turned to Eli for his professional opinion.

"By train robbers? I doubt it." Eli had leaned back slightly in his seat.

"It would be exciting, though, wouldn't it? And I'd be sitting with just the right travel companion." Molly nodded at the pistols Eli wore on his hips.

"And here I was looking forward to a relaxing journey," Eli said with a grin.

Molly returned his smile before letting her gaze flit back to the window. Her imagination was now running rampant with visions of Eli taking down an entire gang of outlaws and whisking her off to safety. She bit her lip to keep from laughing out loud at her fantastic imaginings.

"What will your brother do without you to help at the store?" Eli asked, interrupting her embarrassing train of thought.

She pulled her eyes from the scenery outside the window and sat back, trying to compose herself as if she rode on trains all the time. "He's going to take on the Fitz boy, the eldest one, for the summer."

"The kid's a smart one. He'll do well."

"I hope he will. I felt somewhat badly, leaving my post for so long."

"I'm certain they'll do fine, although you'll be missed. I doubt the Fitz boy will appreciate me bringing him the newspaper."

Molly laughed, and any of the confusion she'd felt about Eli disappeared into a companionable ease. As he pointed out snowcapped mountains in the distance and pronghorn leaping across the terrain, she could hardly tear her eyes from the window. But when she did, she found a friendly face who indulged her excitement. She'd forgotten how easy he was to talk to.

They whiled away the hours in conversation. Eli spoke about some of his more exciting adventures as a sheriff's deputy, including the time he and Sheriff Young rescued the sheriff's sister and future wife from an outlaw with a grudge whose gang had kidnapped them. Molly knew Penny Young well, and could only imagine the trouble she'd given those outlaws. Penny was a lively and outspoken woman, and Molly counted her among her good friends.

Molly didn't have nearly so many exciting stories to tell, but she shared some funny occurrences at the store with Eli. Such as the time she thought she'd heard a pastor's wife ask her to order ten Bibles, when the woman had actually asked for ten bottles. Even though she couldn't bottle cow's milk for orphaned babies with the Bibles, she was able to put those to good use while Molly ordered the bottles.

It was the next morning when they arrived in Denver, and Molly awoke to find the couple seated across from them standing and retrieving their things.

"Good morning," Eli said as he stretched and stood.

"Good morning." A hundred worried thoughts ran through Molly's mind. She'd tried to remain awake, but had failed. She couldn't imagine falling asleep with Eli there across from her, and yet she had. She prayed she didn't look a mess from her upright slumber.

She smoothed her clothing and hair as best she could before rising. And as she did, the worries faded as she realized where she was.

Denver!

Eli retrieved his case and her small valise.

"Thank you," she said as her stomach rumbled. She placed a hand over it, hoping he hadn't heard.

A tiny smile lifted the corner of his mouth. "May I escort you off the train?"

"Please," she said, thankful he'd said nothing about her stomach. "My aunt and uncle should be here to meet me."

Eli led the way down the aisle and off their car to the platform. Molly followed, trying not to get lost in the bustle of people heading to and fro. Aunt Ellen and Uncle John had visited just last year, so at least Molly wasn't searching for people she couldn't recognize. She quickly spotted them near the door to the depot. She pointed, and Eli led her through the crowd toward the building.

Aunt Ellen drew Molly into a hug, welcoming her to Denver. Eli shook hands with Uncle John as Molly made introductions. When Uncle John left to fetch Molly's trunk, Eli handed her the valise.

"Thank you for an eventful journey," he said, that warm smile making her feel as if she'd never left home.

"I don't know if it was that eventful. After all, we ran into no outlaws. I'd hoped to keep your lawman skills from getting too out of practice," she teased.

MOLLY

Eli laughed. "Might I call on you in a few days?"

Molly's heart seemed to stutter to a stop. Call on her? Like a—

"It would be good to see a friendly face," he added, reminding her yet again that that was exactly what she was to him—a friend.

That was why she was here, she chastised herself. To meet men who might see her as more than a "friendly face." In the meantime, it *would* be nice to see Eli. "That would be most welcome," she said.

As he tipped his hat and strode away, Molly found herself sighing. It would be nice to visit with him again, provided she put aside any of the confusing feelings that seemed to arise when he was nearby. After all, she was here to find a man who didn't confuse her in the least.

A man who wanted to marry her.

Chapter Four

ELI COULDN'T BREATHE.

It was incredible how a short, plump woman twenty years his senior could somehow cut off all breath when she hugged him, but Ma was perfectly capable of just that. He pressed her away gently and sucked in a great amount of precious air when she finally let him go.

"I can't believe you're here!" Ma grabbed both his hands and beamed up at him. "It's been so long, I almost forgot I had a son."

"I'm impossible to forget," he said with a grin.

"Hmm, especially with that hair on your chin." She reached up and pinched his chin before he swatted her away. "I don't like that. I always told your father to wear a beard or be clean shaven. Anything in between makes you look like a ruffian."

"I suppose I shouldn't tell you about the pickpocketing I've taken up in my off hours, then?"

Ma shook her head. "You're the spitting image of your father, right down to his sense of humor." She squeezed his hands tight in hers. "I've missed you, my son."

"I've missed you too, Ma."

"Come, eat. I saved you some of the breakfast Mrs. Gowan made. I thought you might be famished after your travels." She led the way through the small house to the kitchen in the rear.

Eli followed gratefully after shedding his coat, hat, and gun belt. Mrs. Gowan, the housekeeper and cook who'd been with Mrs. Jennings since her husband had passed, was putting on a stew to cook for the noon meal. She paused just long enough to hand Eli a covered plate.

"Now," Ma said as she sat in the chair across from him. "Tell me if you have your eye on any young ladies in Cañon City, because Mrs. Graves's daughter is quite free. She isn't particularly charming, or, well . . . much of anything else, but Mrs. Graves says she's adept at setting a table and arranging flowers."

Eli nearly choked on the piece of ham he'd been chewing. He reached for the linen napkin on his lap to cover his mouth.

"As your father always said, a beggar cannot be a chooser. You're twenty-five years old. You have a good job—although quite dangerous. I don't know why you couldn't have gone into business with your father instead. But at least it's respectable and it pays decently. It's high time you took a wife and started a family. Since you're in town, I've taken the liberty of sending a note around to Mrs. Graves—"

"Ma, please! I don't need your help." Eli crushed the napkin into his lap as his mother's eyebrows knitted together. "I'm sorry. I am grateful, it's only that . . . I have a girl I'm sweet on." He said the last words in a rush, and as soon as Ma's face lit up, he wished he could take them back.

"Oh! You do!" She clasped her hands together like a little girl about to receive a candy. "Tell me all about her. What's her name? Where is she from? Who's her family?"

Eli shook his head, desperate for the barrage of questions to end. Behind Ma, Mrs. Gowan hid a grin as she stirred the stew.

"I'll tell you about her later. What I need to know now is more about these debts Pa supposedly owed." He pushed the remainder of the eggs and ham onto his fork.

Ma's face changed instantly. Her fingers traced the edge of the pretty yellow tablecloth in a nervous manner. "The man who's been coming by to collect the payments—he says your father owed his company several business debts."

"Which company?" Eli pushed his plate aside.

"I don't know. The man didn't say."

It was just like his mother not to ask such a thing. "What's the man's name?"

"Mr. Smith," Ma replied, now clasping both hands in her lap.

Eli sighed. There must be scores of men named Smith in Denver. "Did he leave a card, in the event you wanted to find him?"

Ma shook her head.

"The man was quite rude," Mrs. Gowan said as she swooped up Eli's plate and fork.

"He wasn't rude," Ma said, almost defensively. "Only . . . short, I suppose. He speaks as if he's in a hurry. He keeps his buggy waiting out front. It's a fine buggy, too. And he's blue-eyed and quite well-dressed. But always in a hurry."

"Rude," Mrs. Gowan said with a nod at Eli.

"A rude, blue-eyed man named Smith who works for an unknown company, has a fine carriage, and dresses well." Eli wanted to drop his head against the table. "Do you know when he'll be by again?"

"He comes unannounced." Ma stood and pushed her chair under the table.

"Because he's ill-mannered," Mrs. Gowan said under her breath.

Eli bit his lip to keep from smiling at Mrs. Gowan's remark as he stood too. Clearly, she was one who didn't put up with such nonsense as unannounced callers who demanded payment for mystery debts. "Did this Mr. Smith at least tell you how much Pa owed?" Eli asked his mother.

Ma's face drew a pinched look. "That's just it. The first time he visited, he said one thousand. I heard it clear as day."

Eli tried not to wince.

"Then, just a couple of weeks ago, he said 'thousands.' That was when I wrote to you."

An anger traced its way through Eli's veins, burning slowly as he began to piece together this man's ruse. "Did Pa ever say a word about debts?"

"Not a one," Ma replied.

"Took this Mr. Smith nigh on a year to come around, too," Mrs. Gowan added from where she'd moved on to adding flour to some mixture in a bowl.

She was right. None of this made any sense, and if Eli were a gambling man, he'd bet his meager savings that this Mr. Smith was lying through his teeth. All to steal money from a widow. He highly doubted Smith was the man's real name.

Eli pushed his lips together to keep the simmering anger contained. He needed a plan, an investigation of sorts. He'd speak with the city's police, gather names of the most prominent businessmen in town—and the known confidence men, too. He'd ask around, find out if any other widows were being extorted. He'd search through his father's business papers, in case Pa really had owed money. The fire inside eased some, and

Eli felt the strain in his muscles relax. He'd find the truth, one way or another. And if this man was stealing money from his mother, Eli would put him behind bars.

"Now that we have that unpleasantness out of the way, I want to know about this girl you're sweet on." Ma looped her arm through Eli's and led him to the parlor.

Eli's face went warm again. "Ma, can't I get some rest first?"

"Nonsense. It isn't even noon! Who ever heard of taking a rest in the morning?"

"People who slept upright in a train carriage, if I could call it sleeping at all," Eli grumbled.

Ma sat on the worn but comfortable settee she'd had for years. She patted the space next to her and Eli sat, a flood of memories winding their way through his head as he did. Years of listening to his father read the newspaper or the Bible out loud as Eli and his sisters sat comfortably on this very settee. Spying on his eldest sister and her beau holding hands. Telling his parents of his plans to leave Denver to try his luck in Cañon City while they sat here. He hadn't known then that he'd wind up as a lawman. Eli smiled. So many good memories, all bittersweet since the passing of his father.

Ma waited expectantly, for once not saying a word.

Eli sighed. She'd never let him retreat upstairs until he gave her something to satisfy her curiosity. "It isn't as if we're courting," he said, in the vain hope she'd dismiss the entire conversation and let him go.

"Oh? And why not?" Ma narrowed her eyes some, creating tiny wrinkles in her round face. "If she doesn't see you as the finest man she could possibly marry, she isn't worth your time, Eli."

Eli shifted. He'd rather be anywhere and doing anything other than this. Even being held at gunpoint by a madman murderer who'd escaped the federal marshals escorting him to the state penitentiary—which had actually happened a couple of years prior—was preferable to telling his mother about the one woman he wanted but couldn't seem to gather the courage to tell.

"It isn't so much that . . ." he said.

"Good." Ma tilted her head. "Now who is she?"

Eli's eyes drifted longingly to the hallway where the staircase led to two small garret bedrooms upstairs. "Her name is Molly. Molly Hill."

Ma's eyebrows rose at his familiar use of her Christian name.

"I've known her quite a while, Ma. We're friends."

Her eyebrows crested further into her blonde hair, which sat in a swooping style. "Friends? Eli, you aren't taking advantage of this young lady, are you? I raised you—"

"Ma!" Eli rose quickly, hoping to forestall the red he could feel creeping into his face. He paced to the simple fireplace mantel and pretended to study the clock. "No, I'm not . . . taking advantage." He forced himself to take a deep breath before turning around. "It's my job to know everyone in town."

"So you're . . . *friends* with all the ladies in town?" Ma's features twisted in confusion.

"No, not like that. Not . . . *friends*. What does—" He sighed loudly. He didn't even know what he was talking about anymore. "I see her regularly at her family's store. She doesn't know my feelings. That's all I'm trying to say." And he prayed that was enough to satisfy Ma. He took two steps toward the door, indicating *he* thought it should be enough.

But of course it wasn't.

Ma patted the settee again, indicating he should sit. Eli remained where he was. If he was closer to the door, he could make an easier escape.

Ma sighed as if he were causing her great pain by standing so far away. "Are you going to tell me about her, at least? This Miss Hill to whom you can't bring yourself to confess your feelings?"

Eli gritted his teeth. She made it sound so easy. As if it were a simple thing to tell a woman that he found her pretty and interesting and funny. As if it were so easy to ask her what she thought about him. As if it were child's play to get permission from her brother to court her.

All of it made Eli's stomach twist into knots he didn't know how to unravel.

He took another step backwards. "She's pretty. Beautiful, really, with dark hair."

"And?" Ma pressed.

Eli slid backward again. "She's witty. And smart. She enjoys reading the newspaper."

"That's . . . different," Ma said. "The newspaper is full of such dreadful things. I wonder what she sees in it? No mind. Tell me more."

Another step backward and Eli's shoulder hit the doorframe. "She's here in Denver. I might call on her."

That was enough to stun Ma into silence.

He grabbed hold of the opportunity, spinning on his heel and making for the staircase. "I'm going upstairs to lie down for a bit. Tell Mrs. Gowan not to worry about keeping the stew warm for me." And before Ma could say a word, Eli was safely up the stairs and behind the door of his old bedroom.

He sank into the feather bed, grateful for the silence in which to ponder over Ma's situation with this Mr. Smith. And yet, as he drifted off to sleep, it wasn't to thoughts of why he'd come to Denver. It was to images of a sweet, raven-haired girl whose face lit up when she saw him.

Chapter Five

WHILE MOLLY HAD KNOWN Uncle John's work as a banker was lucrative, she hadn't imagined exactly how well-connected her aunt and uncle were. And while it made sense in hindsight—of course Mama had eagerly agreed she come here to stay with them in her pursuit of marriage—Molly wished she'd anticipated it. She'd have brought more dresses, for one: And perhaps spent more time finding new ways to arrange her hair or practicing looking enticing and yet aloof all at the same time.

Yet, it didn't seem any of that was acting to her detriment at this party. Molly wasn't entirely certain what the gathering *was* exactly. Aunt Ellen had mentioned a birthday, and yet there were at least fifty people in attendance in this large house just a mere half a mile from her aunt and uncle's. Aunt Ellen and her friends had taken Molly under their wings, swooping her about the rooms of the house and introducing her to nearly every eligible young man present. Molly had stopped trying to remember names two hours ago.

And now, here she was, seated on an uncomfortable chair in the drawing room, with the attention of no less than five men arranged around her while the lady of the house played a drawn-out tune on the piano situated at the far end of the room.

"Perhaps you'd care for a glass of cold tea?" an eager young man with only half a head of hair asked.

"Oh, no thank you, Mr. . . ." Molly shook her head at the man whose name she'd forgotten.

"Preston," the man supplied, his smile slipping a bit. It made Molly feel badly for not remembering, and she tucked the fact away in her head, hoping not to forget again.

"I've brought you a slice of cake. It's quite delicious—strawberry! My family's company imported the strawberries from California." A handsome man with a spray of freckles across his nose handed her a delicate china plate with a slice of pink cake topped with berries.

Molly smiled at him, wracking her brain for his name. "Thank you, Mr. . . . Carter?"

He bestowed her with a dazzling grin and she congratulated herself on her memory.

"I'll fetch you some lemonade," a Mr. Emerson offered. He was gone before she could say yes or no.

The cake *was* delicious, she decided as she tried a bite. It was almost too perfect to be real. In fact, everything about this house and this entire night was like something out of a dream. The homeowners had family money in steel, her aunt had told her on the short carriage ride to the party. And, Molly surmised once she'd arrived, they hadn't restrained themselves one bit in spending that money. Opulent was the best word she could think of to describe this house. There was nothing like it in Cañon City. A wide, winding staircase, numerous paintings, various pieces of gilt-edged porcelain and china, glittering chandeliers—Molly was certain her mouth hung open the moment she'd walked in the door.

And then there was the party itself. Aunt Ellen had introduced her as the sister of a prominent businessman in Cañon City. If by "prominent," she meant that everyone in town knew Jasper, Molly supposed that was correct. And if by "businessman" she meant Jasper owned a business, that was correct too. However, she suspected these people assumed Jasper owned a home like this and lived as they did. Nothing could be further from the truth.

But even as Molly struggled to remember names, the attention was awfully flattering. She'd wanted for nothing the entire time she was here. But at the same time, it was somewhat overwhelming. She could have laughed at the girl on the train who'd wished for two men to vie for her attention. She'd never imagined five. Or was it six? She could hardly keep track.

Did well-off unmarried ladies who lived here have this happen all the time? Molly wasn't bad looking, but she also wasn't the most beautiful woman in the room. She was smart enough to know she fell solidly in the middle when it came to a pretty face. Maybe it was only because Molly was someone new? It had to be. Well, that and they all thought she came from money.

Mr. Emerson handed her a cold glass of lemonade—with ice! She couldn't imagine how they kept it frozen. Molly peered around Mr. Emerson's eager face and caught Aunt Ellen's eye. Her aunt gave her a secretive smile, and Molly knew she'd been obscure with Molly's background on purpose. She should appreciate her aunt's discretion. After all, wasn't this what she wanted?

If only they weren't so . . . suffocating. The moment Molly finished the last bite of her cake, Mr. Preston (she wouldn't forget the poor man's name now) whisked it away and a Mr. Browning asked if she'd like another slice.

Molly declined, and yet another slice appeared in her hand from yet another man whose name she couldn't remember.

"She said she didn't care for more cake," Mr. Preston sputtered at the man who'd placed the plate in her hand. A third man—Molly couldn't see who it was—retrieved the plate and took it away.

"Perhaps she didn't care for *you* to get it for her," the other man replied.

"Perhaps you ought to go look after your mother. She's appearing less than entertained by Aaronson. You know he's recently widowed?"

The man who'd brought the cake whipped around, and, seemingly having spotted his mother in the crowd of guests, dashed away as the men around Molly laughed.

The laughing settled into an uneasy silence as they returned their attention to her, and Molly wondered what they expected. Was she supposed to be witty? Or bashful? Or flirtatious? It was an uncomfortable feeling she'd never experienced before. She'd hardly ever been shy or at a loss for words around men or women alike, but this wasn't a situation she'd ever truly imagined.

"I . . . I believe I need some air. I feel a bit faint." It wasn't true, despite the fact she'd laced her corset a smidgen tighter than usual. But she did need fresh air—and perhaps a moment or two without feeling as if she were on a stage. She waved her hand at her face to emphasize her point and the men jumped into action.

Before Molly knew what was happening, Mr. Emerson had scooped her up, one arm under her shoulders, the other under her knees, and was carrying her through the crowd. All eyes were on her as the other men pressed people away.

Molly squeezed her eyes shut as her face went warmer than the sun on a hot summer's day. This was the last thing she wanted to happen. Now *everyone* was staring at her. She could only imagine the gossip. They'd likely think her of weak constitution—if they didn't assume she played the part for more attention.

She had to angle her neck just so in order not to be banged against the wall as Mr. Emerson valiantly carried her to a small, empty sitting room in the rear of the house. He laid her on a settee as her entourage surrounded her. Aunt Ellen fluttered through, a hand to her lips when she spied Molly.

Aunt Ellen sat on the edge of the settee and placed the back of her gloved hand against Molly's forehead. "Are you feeling poorly?"

Molly swallowed. She didn't want to lie to her aunt, but she craved a few moments away from all of these men. "I should be fine. Perhaps if I just closed my eyes for a moment?"

Aunt Ellen studied her face, and seemingly satisfied, rose and said, "Of course. Gentlemen, could we give my niece some room? I'm certain she'll return to the festivities shortly." She pressed the men out of the room one-by-one, until Molly was blissfully alone.

She sighed as she leaned back. The chatter and music from the front of the house echoed down the hallway. What in the world was wrong with her? She had what she'd been wanting for so long now. Not a one of those men looked at her like a sister. None of them spoke to her as if she were a friend from their school days. In fact, they eyed her as if she were someone desirable. A woman worthy of courting. They'd even pushed each other aside to be closer to her.

So why wasn't she happy?

Mr. Carter was quite handsome, and Mr. Browning was awfully funny. Even poor Mr. Preston was endearing—she imagined his future wife would mean the world to him. And they were all, she imagined, fairly wealthy.

And yet none of them held her attention. In the back of her mind, she compared Mr. Emerson's bright blue eyes to the soulful hazel of Eli Jennings's. And while Mr. Browning made her laugh, it wasn't as thorough as the way she'd laughed at the stories Eli had shared with her on the journey to Denver.

Molly leaned her head back on the settee, likely mussing the hair Aunt Ellen's personal maid had spent the better part of an hour on. What was she doing? Since when had Eli Jennings become the measure of everything a man should be? Eli—the man she'd thought for a handful of days might have feelings for her. But he didn't. And it was silly to think otherwise, when he'd had months to act on them and hadn't.

No, he was just like the others back home. She was a friendly face—he'd said just as much to her only two days ago when they arrived. She'd do well to remember that.

Molly sat for a few more moments, resolving to give these men a fair chance. She'd come here to meet a beau, after all.

And yet as she returned to the party, she wondered what Eli would think of all of this. What would he say about the California strawberries, the grand piano, the gilded stemware—and the men who crowded around her as if she were European royalty?

Chapter Six

FOUR DAYS HAD GOTTEN Eli drawers of his father's papers, one quick chat with a police officer, a handful of names, and approximately six hundred nudges from his mother to call on Molly.

And so here he was, standing outside her aunt and uncle's fine home on 14th Street, at eleven o'clock. He raised his hand to knock on the door, but it opened for him, revealing a staid-looking man in a plain black suit. Eli swallowed, feeling suddenly far out of place. Molly hadn't mentioned that her relatives lived in a house this large, or that they apparently employed a butler. He tugged on his collar and cleared his throat. "I'm Eli Jennings, here to call on Miss Hill."

"She is expecting you." The man pulled the door open fully and Eli stepped into a roomy entryway. He glanced about as the man took his coat and hat. He was glad he'd left his guns behind at Ma's; he couldn't imagine the look this man might give him if he'd walked into this house with them on.

As the butler led him into a comfortable-looking parlor, Eli took in his surroundings. Nothing about this house, aside from its size and location, said the Blanchets were moneyed. In fact, it felt like his mother's house—warm and welcoming. A fire burned in the fireplace, a handmade quilt dressed the simple settee, and two inviting chairs were arranged at a conversational angle. One of them contained a gray striped cat, curled into a ball and fast asleep. Eli smiled. This was the sort of room a man could feel at home in.

A throat cleared behind him, and Eli turned to see the butler with Molly beside him. "May I present Miss Hill?" the man said formally, as if Eli and Molly had never met. "Shall I ask Rosa to bring you refreshments?"

Molly glanced at Eli, who shook his head. "No, thank you. Please, Eli, sit. Uncle John is at the bank, and Aunt Ellen will be down shortly."

The butler lingered a half-moment longer, eyeing Eli as if he didn't quite trust him before finally disappearing from the room. Eli took the chair unoccupied by the cat, while Molly settled herself on the settee, carefully arranging a yellow-and-white-striped dress that made him think of a summer's day by the Arkansas River back home. The thought warmed him, and when Molly glanced up and caught his expression with her soft brown eyes, Eli pulled at his collar again, wishing it weren't so tight.

"Is the fire too much? Should I ask to have it extinguished?" she asked.

"No, it's fine. It was the walk," Eli said quickly. "After the horsecar ride, that is. I had to walk a small distance." He searched for something to change the subject. "How are you finding Denver?"

Molly's smile lit up the room more than the fire burning nearby. "It's wonderful! I never could have imagined how big it is. I've seen the horse railroad from the carriage. It's magnificent, the horses pulling along the trolley on the tracks like that. Can you imagine if Cañon City grew large enough to need such a thing? And how many people there are! We attended a gathering the other evening for a birthday, and it was more like a . . . I don't know. There were far more people there than for any other birthday celebration I've ever attended. And the house! Eli, you should have seen this house. It was magnificent. There is nothing like it in Cañon City. It even made the McClure Hotel look small and unimpressive."

Her enthusiasm bubbled like the river during the spring melt, and it was impossible not to smile along with her. "Your aunt and uncle's home is very fine itself."

"It is, but not to the extent of the house we visited." She leaned forward and lowered her voice, as if she were telling him a secret. "Their silverware wasn't silver. It was gold! Can you imagine?"

"I cannot." Her awe made him bite his lip to keep from smiling too much.

"Tell me, what have you been doing these past few days?" Molly asked, her hands clasped.

Eli sat back in the comfortable chair. "Helping my mother."

"Oh? Has she put you to work?"

"Not in so many words." He paused. It might help to unburden himself of the debt dilemma. Perhaps if he spoke of it aloud to someone who knew neither his father nor his mother, some of the confusion might lift. "My father ran a lumberyard while he was alive. It did fine—not as impressive as, well . . ." He glanced about the room. "Anyhow, a couple of months ago, a man came to visit my mother." He told Molly what he'd learned from Ma.

"Do you think he was telling the truth?" Molly asked, her eyebrows knitted in concern.

"I don't know," Eli said. "I suspect he wasn't, but I don't know for certain. Not yet. I've gone through some of my father's papers, spoken with the city police, and gathered the names of a few men with whom he did business. I'm hoping to find a way to meet these men in the coming days. But I've turned up no evidence of any debts and no dealings with anyone named Smith. I suspect Smith isn't the man's real name. This evening—"

"Oh, there you are!" Molly's aunt swooped into the room, a friendly smile on her face and her hands reaching for Eli's the moment he stood. "I am so happy you came to call on our Molly. Visiting a new place is wonderful, but it's always comforting to see a friend from home. How marvelous to see you again, Mr. Jennings."

"He's a deputy, Auntie," Molly said as her aunt scooped up the cat and took its place in the other chair.

"Oh, yes! I'd forgotten. A man of the law. That must be very exciting!" Mrs. Blanchet said as she settled the cat into her lap. "Molly told me all about how you rescued a dear friend of hers from a terrible outlaw."

A rush of heat flooded Eli from head to toe. Molly had been speaking to her aunt about him. "Well, I don't know that I—"

"Now, don't be humble about it. It's quite impressive." Mrs. Blanchet barely took a breath before turning to Molly. "That's a lovely color on you, my dear. Don't you think so, Mr.—I'm sorry, Deputy?"

Eli was certain his face was the same shade as the red flowers that sat in a vase on the table to the left of his chair. And if he'd observed correctly, Molly's face was pinker than it had been also. "You don't have to call me that. I hold no local—"

"Pssh." Mrs. Blanchet waved a hand at him. "Isn't yellow a lovely color on her?"

"Yes," Eli said, although it felt as if he had to fight a nest of snakes in his throat to get the word out. Not that he *didn't* think Molly looked beautiful. He found her radiant in whatever color she wore. But he'd never said so. He'd never had the courage to say so.

"Although Mr. Emerson was quite taken with the red silk you had on the other night," Mrs. Blanchet said, her attention entirely on Molly. "He told Mrs. Peabody so, and she mentioned it to me at tea yesterday."

A zing of irritation rolled through Eli. His gaze shot to Molly, who smiled at her aunt. Somehow, that smile was more painful than Mrs. Blanchet's words.

"Our Molly was quite the belle of the ball. Several young men of standing have asked to call on her." Mrs. Blanchet looked at Molly approvingly as Eli tapped his hand against his knee. A sudden restlessness made it hard for him to remain seated. He didn't know what he wanted to do, but sitting here and listening to Molly's aunt fawn over how popular her niece was with the eligible men in town certainly was *not* it.

"Auntie," Molly said, her eyes on her hands.

Eli burned to know how many men were coming to call on Molly, and when, precisely, so he could . . . what, exactly? Push them out of the way and command her attention all to himself?

He pressed his nails into the palms of his hands.

"Now, Deputy, have you any social plans while you're in town? Are you attending the Lucketts' soiree by chance? Or the dance at the Prestons'? They always have such lovely balls." Mrs. Blanchet watched him now.

Eli forced his hands to relax. "I'm not acquainted with those families, I'm afraid." Although . . . "You wouldn't be speaking about Gregory Preston? Of Preston Timber and Logging?"

"Yes! He's the eldest son in the family. I take it you're acquainted with Mr. Preston, then?" Mrs. Blanchet beamed.

"Yes, well, no . . ." Preston's name was on the short list he'd compiled of men who had done business with his father. If he could wrangle an invitation to this gathering, it would save him time in needing to track the man down at his office in town. "I'd like to meet him," Eli said honestly. "For business purposes."

"Ah, well, then you must come to the dance!"

Eli sat up straighter. Had it really been that easy? "Are you certain? The Prestons don't know me and—"

Mrs. Blanchet waved a hand at him again. "They won't mind a whit. I'll tell them you're our guest."

Eli snuck a glance at Molly. She gave him an encouraging smile and he tried not to wonder too much if that meant she was happy he'd be attending the dance.

"If you're looking to make business connections, you'll meet many of our city's finest businessmen at the Prestons'. You ought to sit down with my husband also. I'm certain he could help you."

"That's very kind, thank you. I'll let you know." Mr. Blanchet, thankfully, was not on Eli's list, and he hoped his answer was satisfactory to Mrs. Blanchet. The last thing he wanted to look to Molly's aunt was ungrateful.

Mrs. Blanchet shooed the cat from her lap and stood. "I'm afraid I must go see to the preparations for dinner. It was wonderful to see you, Deputy." She took his hand as he stood and squeezed it. "Please do come around again."

Eli thanked her for her generosity. He hoped for a few more moments with Molly for time to . . . what? Just the idea of telling her how he felt about her made it feel as if his tongue had swollen to three times its size. But he needed to do something, *say* something, to her before he missed his chance completely.

Molly stood also, smoothing the striped skirt she wore. Eli wished he could remember to compliment her on such things as skirts or hats. She might like that.

Molly moved toward the door, and Eli followed her. She paused by a table topped with lace and turned to face him. "I am so happy you're going to the Prestons'. It will be so much less . . . suffocating with you there."

Eli had no idea what she meant, but her words brought a smile to his face. She was happy he'd be there—that was all he needed to hear. He tried to be sensible and not to read too much into it, but sense was something that frittered around the edges of his mind at the moment.

"Might I call on you again?" he asked.

Molly tilted her head, her eyes narrowing just slightly, as if what he'd said confused her. "Of course. Please let me know how you progress with your mother's problem."

"I will. It happens that Gregory Preston is one of the men my father regularly did business with."

"Oh? What a happy coincidence!" The barest touch of a frown tugged the corners of her mouth down, but it was gone before Eli could be certain it was ever there to begin with.

"I'll see you soon," he said. And before he could convince himself not to do it, he'd taken her hand and placed a kiss on the back of it. Her hand was small and delicate in his own, and her skin warm against his lips.

"Good afternoon, Eli," she said softly as she withdrew her hand.

When he took his leave, she was smiling. Perhaps he did stand a fighting chance against the Mr. Prestons of Denver, after all.

Chapter Seven

"IT'S OF PRIMARY IMPORTANCE that the berries arrive as quickly as possible, else they go bad before reaching tables here in Denver. Now oranges..." Mr. Carter droned on about the oranges his family's company imported from California.

Molly glanced out the carriage window. Rain continued to lash the sides of the Brougham. It had been cloudy when they left her aunt and uncle's home, but dry. Else she never would have agreed to a drive with the tedious Mr. Carter. Of course, she also hadn't realized exactly how dull the man was before stepping into a carriage with him. He was striking with his blond hair and freckles, but his personality was as bland as a bowl of mush.

"Now, my sister insisted we continue purchasing apples from the orchards outside the city, and I must say, she was correct. Colorado apples are quite popular and..."

Could he not see how bored she was? The man must be completely oblivious to the frown on her face or the way her eyes kept drifting to the windows or her unsuccessful attempts at changing the subject. Mr. Carter was not the first male caller she'd had since the birthday celebration last week, but he was certainly the least interesting.

Her gaze found the window again as Mr. Carter shifted next to her. They had paused nearby a row of retail establishments. Several carriages—many of them identical to Mr. Carter's—lined the road. Well-dressed ladies scurried to the waiting buggies while their male companions and drivers carried packages. A few gentlemen hurried down the wooden walkway in front of the businesses. As she watched, a tall man with a worn brown hat exited what looked like a lawyer's office. Molly squinted at the words painted on the window. Yes, it was a lawyer's office. And the man . . . She squinted again as he looked up into the rain. It was Eli!

Her heart began beating faster and her fingers tingled as if she was nervous about something. Why should she feel anxious to see Eli? If anything, she ought to feel relieved, as this gave her the perfect opportunity to not only help a friend, but relieve her own boredom.

"Mr. Carter!" She interrupted the man as he soliloquized on the virtues of peaches. "We must rescue Mr. Jennings from this rain." Without waiting for his response, she opened the door of the Brougham and leaned out just far enough to call for him.

Eli glanced up, and after a moment of searching for the source of his name, spotted her.

"Mr. Jennings!" she called. It felt strange to speak to him so formally, but shouting his Christian name across the boardwalk would likely send tongues wagging about the two of them all across town. "Please, come in out of the rain."

He moved toward the carriage as Mr. Carter looked on curiously.

Molly scooted back as he entered, the rain dripping from his hat and coat. Too late, she realized the Brougham had only the one wide seat. But that didn't seem to faze Eli, who pulled

MOLLY   45

down a retractable seat directly across from Molly. It looked as if it were made for a child, and Eli had to twist his legs to the side to fit.

"Thank you. I apologize for my appearance," he said as he settled himself as best he could on the tiny seat. Mr. Carter nodded. He was too well-bred to say anything despite the disapproving look on his face.

Molly could have reached across the inch or so separating them and wrapped Eli in a hug, wet coat and all. He had no idea how he was saving her. Conversation could never be dull with Eli.

"Mr. Carter, please meet Deputy Jennings of Cañon City. Deputy, this is Mr. Carter. His family owns a fruit company." The latter fact was the only piece of information she knew about Mr. Carter besides the fact he had a sister. He'd spoken of nothing else for the past thirty minutes.

"Deputy?" Mr. Carter's eyebrows were raised. At last something besides fruit had finally intrigued him—a feat Molly apparently couldn't accomplish on her own.

"Yes, to the Fremont County sheriff." Eli removed his hat and set it in his lap. He ran his fingers through his hair, and Molly was seized by the oddest desire to do the same thing.

She clasped her hands in their tea-colored silk gloves together, immediately remembering—for approximately the hundredth time—the way Eli had kissed her hand before leaving a couple of days ago. He was being polite, she reminded herself again. He'd had plenty of opportunities to make any feelings he had for her known—and he hadn't. There was no reason for her to believe otherwise now. He was a friend to her and nothing more. She'd do well to rein in these strange reactions she'd been having to him lately, lest she find herself leaving Denver with nothing but a broken heart.

No, she needed to place her attention on the men she was meeting here. She pursed her lips as she looked at Mr. Carter. Perhaps not on him, though. He'd bore her into an early grave.

"How interesting," Mr. Carter said. "It seems like something out of the dreams of a young boy."

It was an underhanded compliment, and Mr. Carter knew it. Molly fixed him with a frown, but Eli seemed to take it in stride.

"I didn't necessarily dream of chasing down drunks or settling disputes between shopkeepers, but otherwise it is, as you say, interesting." Eli had an amused look to his face as he spoke. He glanced at Molly, who bit back a grin.

Mr. Carter's eyes narrowed, but only for a split second before he returned his attention to Molly. "Miss Hill, perhaps you'd enjoy a drive out to one of the orchards from which we purchase various sorts of fruit."

Molly could think of nothing she wanted to do less. "I . . . regret that my social calendar may be full." She gave him a smile that she hoped lessened the blow.

But Mr. Carter was undeterred. "Next week might do. Mornings would be best. Surely you have a morning or two free?"

Equal parts irritation and guilt rose inside Molly. Why couldn't he see she wasn't interested? And was she a terrible person for lying so to him? "My mornings, well . . ." She trailed off, searching in vain for an excuse that might spare the man's feelings.

"I fear I've already engaged her with entertaining my mother each morning. She's a widow and desires company more than anything. I'm certain you understand," Eli said.

Molly gaped at him. It was an outright lie, unless... Did he *want* her to spend time with his mother? If so, why?

"I see," Mr. Carter said, his eyebrows raised and a slice of annoyance in his voice as he regarded Molly. "Perhaps one afternoon, then. I can come fetch you about two o'clock. Let's say Monday?"

Molly glanced down at her hands. She'd never been in such a situation. What could she say? She didn't want to hurt Mr. Carter's feelings, and yet, letting him believe he stood a chance in courting her was just as cruel. When she looked up, still uncertain how to turn Mr. Carter down, she found Eli watching her. He nodded ever so slightly before turning to Mr. Carter.

"Sir, I believe the lady is uninterested in visiting your orchards. Perhaps you might take another young lady of your acquaintance?"

Molly let out a breath and thanked God with every fiber of her being that Eli was here and had the perfect words to say to Mr. Carter.

However, it seemed Mr. Carter did not agree with her assessment.

"Pardon me?" he said, bristling like an angry cat. "That isn't at all what she said. Was it, Miss Hill?"

Molly didn't have a chance to reply. Eli straightened in his seat, as best he could, and looked Mr. Carter right in the eye. "It was, and I'd advise you to place your attentions elsewhere or you won't like what happens next."

Molly's eyes widened at Eli's words, even as a flush of pride rose through her. *This* was why he was a lawman. And he was here, protecting her.

"Are you threatening me?" Mr. Carter's chest puffed out and his blue-gray eyes grew stormy.

"I'm doing no such thing," Eli said with a smile. "Provided you accept Miss Hill's decision like a gentleman."

Mr. Carter gripped the seams of his jacket and pulled on them as he sat back. Molly had the distinct impression no one had ever talked to him like that before.

It was only a few strained, silent moments before they arrived at Aunt Ellen and Uncle John's home. Molly mostly kept her eyes on the window, but occasionally shot looks at Eli, who gave her a reassuring grin.

"Good day, Mr. Carter," Molly said before accepting Eli's hand to exit the Brougham. "Thank you for the drive."

"You're very welcome," he said in a strained voice. He didn't attempt to help her out himself. In fact, it seemed to take every ounce of energy he had just to nod to her before she stepped out.

Eli took her by the elbow and led her to the front door as the rain fell steadily around them.

"Thank you," she said once they arrived. "For deterring him."

"I'm happy to scare away all other suitors you may wish to have removed from your presence," he said, his eyes a merry green even in the gray rain. His hand hadn't moved from her elbow and Molly found herself acutely aware of his touch.

Molly laughed. "Perhaps not all of them." The words came out more teasing than she'd intended. And as a muscle twitched in Eli's jaw, she wondered why she'd said such a thing. She wasn't trying to make Eli jealous . . . was she? No, not only was that utterly pointless, but she wasn't that sort of a girl.

Not that she'd ever had the *opportunity* to be that sort of a girl.

Molly glanced out at the rain, trying to stop the thoughts from tumbling through her head. "How will you get home? Would you like me to see if Uncle John's driver will take you?"

"I'll walk to the horsecar." The intense look faded from Eli's eyes as he smiled softly. "I promise a little rain won't hurt me."

"Are you certain? Perhaps you'd rather come in for a while?"

"I hate to turn down such an invitation, but Ma is waiting on me to bring her purchases." He patted the pocket of his coat where Molly assumed he'd put the items he'd bought.

"All right. I'll see you on Saturday, then, for the dance."

"Saturday," he said, finally releasing her elbow to tip his hat. "I'll look forward to it as I never have anything else." And with a smile, he made his way down the steps to the sidewalk.

Molly waited at the door despite the rain dripping from her hat until he was gone from her sight. As she entered the house, she found herself looking forward to Saturday too. But it wasn't the bevy of suitors she might find there that played through her thoughts.

It was Eli.

Chapter Eight

COMING TO THIS DANCE had been a bad idea.

Eli shifted uncomfortably in the corner of the Prestons' large ballroom. When one of the family's servants walked by with glasses of cold tea with chips of ice, he accepted one, if only to have something with which to occupy his hands. He'd hoped to accomplish two things tonight: speaking with a number of the men whose names were on the list he'd made and spending more time with Molly. But he hadn't managed introductions to more than one of the men, whom he immediately dismissed as a suspect when he learned the man had sold his business for a pretty penny last fall. And Molly sat surrounded by a bevy of suitors, unreachable and—he feared—unattainable. Mr. Carter, he'd noticed, was clear across the room, trying to gain the attention of two other ladies.

He downed the tea in two gulps and set the empty glass on a table. It was ridiculous hiding here in the corner and feeling sorry for himself. He spotted the younger Mr. Preston on the fringes of the men surrounding Molly. He ran the logging and timber business he'd put together with his brothers, and then subsequently bought them out. He would be useful to speak with. And maybe he'd get a word in edgewise with Molly.

Determined, Eli strode across the room, weaving between groups of men and ladies in conversation and dodging a dancing couple whose exuberance had nearly sent them crashing into the people surrounding the dance floor.

"How is your ankle, Miss Hill? Are you certain you don't need to lie down?" one of the men was asking Molly when Eli arrived.

He sidled in between Preston and a rather large fellow who watched Molly as if she weren't quite real.

"Oh, no. It's much better, thank you," Molly said. She *didn't* look quite real, not in that brilliant emerald dress and with the way her hair sat softly around her face. She looked instead like a painting, as if an artist's imagination had come to life.

"Would you care to dance, then?" Preston asked, peering around the man in front of him.

"I'd love to, but perhaps in a few minutes? I ought to rest it a bit longer." Molly turned a tight yet somehow still dazzling smile at Preston. But when her eyes landed on Eli, the tightness disappeared.

Eli stood straighter, his heart soaring at the fact that she seemed truly happy to see him. "Good evening again, Miss Hill," he said formally.

"I'd wondered where you'd gotten off to." Molly stood, ankle seemingly forgotten. "Gentlemen, this is a dear friend of mine from home—"

"Eli Jennings," Eli said before she could identify his line of work. He figured he might get farther in his conversations with the men his father had done business with if they didn't think he was investigating them on behalf of the law. The men nodded at him, some introducing themselves. When Eli finally turned back toward Molly, she was engaged in conversation with a Mr. Browning. Her smile appeared forced again, however, and that was enough to satisfy Eli. Now if he could only figure out how to engage Preston in conversation enough to determine if he knew anything about the supposed debts Eli's father owed.

"Jennings," Preston mused next to him. "Are you by chance related to the late Theodore Jennings? The one who ran the lumberyard?"

Or perhaps this wouldn't be hard at all. "Yes, he was my father. I believe he might have done some business with your company?"

"Indeed—" Preston stopped speaking as something over Eli's shoulder caught his eye.

Eli turned, following Preston's line of sight until his eyes landed on Molly, dancing a waltz with the man called Browning. Jealousy snaked its way through Eli. He tried to shrug it off. Molly could dance with whomever she chose, after all. But he couldn't shake the envy. More than anything, Eli wanted it to be *him* she chose to dance with.

Of course, that meant he'd need to ask her.

"That snake," Preston said as he watched the couple. "He knew I had the next dance with her." The man's eyes narrowed as he took in the people surrounding them in the ballroom. They landed on a pair of ladies—sisters by the looks of them—standing nearby. "Come," he said to Eli.

Not entirely certain what they were doing, Eli followed the few steps to where the sisters stood. He needed only a few more moments with Preston. Maybe after he'd finished his chat with these women, Eli could find out more about his father's business dealings with Preston's company.

MOLLY 53

"Ladies, might I introduce Mr. Jennings?" Preston said, a winning smile on his face and his dark blue eyes twinkling even as the light in the room reflected off his half-bald pate. "Mr. Jennings, this is Miss Tucker and Miss Tucker. Their father is in the state government."

"Pleased to meet you," Eli said. The girls smiled at him, one hiding her face behind a fan. They were tall and willowy, with hair the color of sand and complexions that looked as if they'd never seen the sun.

"Would you ladies like to dance?" Preston held out a hand to the nearest sister as if she would never consider saying no. And she didn't, taking his hand.

"I'd love to," the second sister said, glancing up from her fan to Eli.

This wasn't what he'd wanted to do. In fact, he'd hoped he could make it through this event without dancing at all—except perhaps with Molly. But now this young lady was looking at him with expectant eyes. To decline after Preston so much as asked for him would be the height of rudeness, and so Eli took Miss Tucker's hand and led her to the dance floor.

Around they went, Miss Tucker trying valiantly to keep the conversation going and Eli's eyes constantly finding Molly. Did she look happy? He couldn't tell from this distance.

"Did you try the mint ice cream?" Miss Tucker asked, her fan bumping his arm from where it hung about her wrist. "It's divine."

"I haven't," Eli replied. They were a little closer to Molly and her dance partner now. Eli furrowed his forehead as he watched them. She was not smiling as most of the ladies dancing were. Browning had leaned forward and was whispering in her ear.

Eli ground his teeth together. What was he saying to her?

The waltz took Molly out of his line of vision. But as soon as they turned again, his eyes found her right away. She was shaking her head at Browning, the frown still fixed on her face. It wasn't like Molly to look so upset during conversation. She was kind to everyone; it was something he admired about her.

"Mr. Jennings? Is something the matter?" Miss Tucker was looking in Molly's direction too.

"I'm afraid it is." And just as the words left his mouth, Molly pushed a hand against Browning's chest. Eli twisted his head to see Browning cling even tighter to Molly's other hand and her waist. Anger as hot as blue fire tore through Eli.

"Pardon me," he said through a clenched jaw to Miss Tucker. It was as if he'd lost all control of his actions as he strode toward Molly and Browning. He pushed in between them, and without a second thought, he raised a fist and landed it square against Browning's jaw.

Chapter Nine

MOLLY GASPED. WHERE had Eli come from? Mr. Browning reeled backward, narrowly missing another dancing couple, a hand flying to his jaw. And Eli stood there, in front of Molly, his fist poised to strike again.

The music continued to play, but the other dancers had begun to form a circle around them. Snippets of their words floated to Molly's ears.

"What happened?"

"Did he hit Browning?"

"Who is that?"

But Molly's attention remained on Eli, who kept her shielded from Mr. Browning—the man who'd gone from friendly to forceful when he suggested they converse in another room and she'd declined. Eli had seen her fear, somehow. And now here he was, ready to defend her again.

Ready to become the subject of gossip among all of Denver's finest families.

Molly took a step forward, reaching for his outstretched arm. "Eli—"

"What was that about?" Mr. Browning had apparently recovered from the blow. Molly peered around Eli to see the man stepping forward, a hand to his jaw still.

"You know." Eli spoke as if he'd swallowed pebbles.

Mr. Browning dropped his hand as he worked his jaw. "You misunderstood, although I appreciate your intentions. I promise nothing was amiss." He glanced at the people surrounding them, quiet especially now that the music had stopped. "Nothing was amiss," he announced again.

Bits of quiet chatter arose, but the crowd did not disperse. And Eli didn't move a muscle.

Mr. Browning eyed Eli's fist, which was still raised. "A dance with ladies is no place for fisticuffs."

Molly couldn't see around Eli, but from his quick, steady breathing, she imagined he was making a decision. She prayed it was the right one. "Eli," she said in a voice meant for his ears only. She wanted to place a hand on his arm, but she couldn't—not unless she wanted to send tongues wagging more than they already would.

The seconds ticked by, and, slowly, he lowered his hand. He stepped forward. Mr. Browning flinched, but glancing at those watching, held his ground. He offered Eli a nervous smile.

"You so much as speak to Miss Hill again, I promise I'll pick this up where we left off," Eli said in a low voice.

"You would do well not to threaten me," Mr. Browning replied, in a voice barely audible to Molly, much less the others around them. "But you needn't worry. My interest in Miss Hill has waned considerably."

Molly had never heard such beautiful words.

Eli eyed Browning for a moment before turning suddenly and stalking through the crowd. Molly went to follow him, only to run into her aunt's outstretched arm.

"Give him a moment," Aunt Ellen said as the music and dancing resumed.

MOLLY

Molly nodded, her breath caught in her throat as she watched Eli disappear from the room.

"Did that man hurt you?" her aunt asked, assessing Molly as if evidence would be visible on her dress or her face. "I can't imagine Mr. Jennings overreacting in such a way. He doesn't seem the sort."

"He didn't." Molly tore her eyes from the door. "Mr. Browning was rather insistent I join him alone in another room."

Aunt Ellen's eyes narrowed. "He's a scoundrel. And I'll ensure his mother hears of it. Come, you need a refreshment after that excitement."

Molly stayed close to her aunt's side for the next hour, declining dance invitations from the other men who hovered nearby. Aunt Ellen shooed them away, claiming Molly needed time to recover from the events of the evening. Molly was grateful. The last thing she could imagine right now was dancing, especially when she yearned to find Eli and thank him.

Finally, he reappeared in the ballroom. He kept near the wall, out of sight from party guests who would want to know more about what had happened.

Molly looked to her aunt, who nodded.

Molly gave her a grateful smile before walking around where most of the guests had gathered on her way to Eli.

"Molly," he said when he saw her, a smile alighting his face. "Are you all right?"

"I am, thanks to you." She paused in front of him as laughter sounded nearby. Another couple was just beyond them. "Might we go elsewhere?"

Eli nodded. "Better than becoming the talk of the town." He slipped out the ballroom door, and after glancing about to ensure no one was watching, Molly followed.

Silently, Eli led the way downstairs. He peeked into rooms, but others occupied them already. "Outside?" he asked.

Molly nodded, and he pushed open the front door. The house was set back some from the road, with a small garden not yet in bloom and a pretty cast-iron gate at the street. When Molly had first arrived that evening, she thought she'd been transported away from Denver to some large city in the East.

There was a chill in the night air, as usual, and Molly wished she had her coat. At least the cool air kept everyone else inside.

"Here." Eli removed his jacket and laid it around Molly's bare shoulders.

"Thank you." She snuggled into the coat. Not only was it warm, it also smelled of Eli—a mix of leather and freshly cut timber. She wanted to burrow her face into it, but settled instead for drawing it closely around her. "For both the coat and for rescuing me—again."

He grimaced and gestured at a small iron bench that sat in the garden. "I shouldn't have reacted in such a way."

"You saved me from that lout," Molly said as she sat on the bench. "His jaw will heal. Although I'm not sure his pride will."

"I doubt I'll be welcome at another one of these soirees," Eli said, sitting next to her. "It's just as well. I'm finding it rather tedious."

Molly hid a smile behind the collar of Eli's coat. "That's too bad. You were the most interesting person in that ballroom."

He raised his eyebrows. "I doubt that. After all, Mr. Carter enraptured you with his discussions of fruit orchards the other day."

"True," Molly said, unable to keep the giggle from her lips.

Eli smiled too, for a moment, before looking more serious. "At least Browning isn't one of the men I need to speak with. I wouldn't get a word out of him now. I fear the others won't talk to me either."

Molly's heart felt as if someone had pricked it with a needle. He might have messed up any chance he had at figuring out who his father owed money to—all because of her. "I'm so sorry."

Eli laid a hand on top of hers. "You have no need to apologize. What happened was not your fault, and I'm glad I was there to set him to rights."

She swallowed hard and glanced down at his hand. He was being friendly . . . wasn't he? Then why did she want so badly to turn her own hand so her palm would be facing his?

"Molly?"

She glanced up to find him watching her, a lock of his hair hanging in his eye, freed from the grease he must have used to keep the rest of his hair back. She smiled at it and, without letting herself think, reached up and brushed it back with her other hand. When she drew her hand away, she realized what she'd done. Warmth began to spread across her face. "I'm sorry," she said quickly.

"Don't be. That hair has been giving me fits all evening. It ought to be in fashion to wear a hat during these sorts of things," he said with an impish grin.

She returned his smile, but her heart beat a little faster as she tried to puzzle out what exactly was happening. She withdrew her hand from under his in an effort to force her thoughts to assemble themselves into something that made sense.

Eli straightened, tugging at his vest, and that stubborn piece of hair fell into his eyes again. He brushed it away, and Molly bit her lip to keep from laughing.

"I might have an idea," she said. Now that he wasn't so close, she could think again.

"About . . . ?"

"Your situation. But I need to think through it some more." She pulled her hands inside the sleeves of his jacket to keep them warm as she waited for his response.

"All right. Might I call on you again, then? To discuss it in more detail," he added in a hurry.

"Of course, please do." Her heart felt strangely light, as if it might dance off on its own. "We ought to return to the party, before anyone misses us."

"I doubt anyone will miss me," he said with a crooked grin. And as he reached for her hand to help her up, Molly had one thought.

She would miss him.

Chapter Ten

ON TUESDAY MORNING, Eli found himself facing down the Blanchets' dour butler again. He wondered if the man was capable of a smile. He'd be excellent in a game of cards. Eli declined being escorted to the parlor and kept his coat and hat; he had another plan for today.

Molly, in contrast to the butler, was a ray of sunshine when she descended the stairs. She wore a light blue dress without much ornamentation, but it wasn't needed. The color was beautiful, but it was no comparison to the genuine smile that lit her face when she saw Eli.

She paused at the bottom of the stairs and glanced at the butler. "Thank you, Stevens."

The butler nodded and disappeared into the rear of the house, leaving them alone in the foyer.

"Good afternoon, Eli," Molly said, her hand resting lightly on the intricately carved newel. "Aunt Ellen sends her greetings. She had another appointment today." Molly paused. "I imagined I would find you in the parlor."

Eli tapped his hat against his thigh. "I thought we might go for a stroll."

Molly's smile brightened her face all over again. Eli decided he might not mind standing here all day, just watching how such a small motion as a smile could lend a twinkle to her eyes and make a tiny dimple in her cheek come to life.

"What a wonderful idea. Let me retrieve my things, and we can go." Molly swept past him, a rush of lavender. Eli wanted to close his eyes and breathe in the scent, or better yet, pull her into his arms. But he held firm, fingers gripping his hat so hard he feared he might dent it.

Molly returned, wrapped in a navy cloak with a matching hat tilted just so on her head. Eli led the way down the front steps to the sidewalk, where he offered her an arm. Molly took it, her eyes grazing his face just briefly before turning forward again. What he wouldn't give to have her looking up at him like that all the time.

Eli clenched his jaw. His head was running off on flights of fancy. He needed to remain here, in this moment. First to discover what her idea was regarding his mother's situation, and second . . . to find out if what he thought he saw in her expression or heard in her voice at the dance Saturday night was still there. Because for a moment, it seemed she might be seeing him the way he'd hoped for so long. If her voice went soft again, or if she regarded him as if he were the only man around as she did in the garden, he resolved to finally speak the words he'd been wanting to say for nearly a year.

"Shall we walk toward town?" Molly asked.

Eli nodded, and they turned right. Eli tried to push thoughts of her smile and her sweet voice to the back of his mind, so he could concentrate on something that didn't involve his heart—his father's supposed debts. "Might now be the time you enlighten me about your idea for my mother's situation?"

MOLLY

Molly looked up at him, excitement dancing in her dark eyes, which made all of those thoughts he'd tried to set aside threaten to consume him all over again. "Yes, I believe I could be of some help."

Eli guided her around a crate that had been placed on the walkway in front of a house. "How is that?"

"What are the names of the men with whom you need to speak?"

"A Mr. Robert Trumball, Mr. Clinton Edwards, Mr. George Emerson, and Preston, of course. I didn't get to talk with him about matters of business on Saturday."

"Well . . . some of the men with whom you need to speak have some interest in . . ." She trailed off, chewing her lip, and then forged ahead. "They were among the men who wanted to dance with me Saturday evening."

"Oh." The knowledge thumped Eli against the skull. He knew that—of course he did, he was there, after all. But the reminder pinched like a bee sting.

"And so, I thought I could use my . . . standing with them to learn more for you. Well, three of them, anyway. Mr. Trumball is an elderly gentleman."

"You want to interrogate your beaux on my behalf," Eli said before he could carve the bluntness from his words. It was unlike him, to speak so plainly with Molly, and yet it was as if he couldn't keep it inside.

"They aren't my *beaux*," Molly said, a tiny smile curving the ends of her lips. "And yes, since I have an audience with them, why shouldn't I use that to help a friend?"

A friend. The words were like a smack in the face. Had he imagined all that had happened Saturday night, then? Eli's head was muddled, and all he wanted to do was dunk it in a trough of cold water to clear the confusion.

"Yes," he finally said, the word strained. "I'd be deeply grateful for whatever information you might be able to find."

Molly beamed at him, seemingly oblivious to how hard it was for him to even get the words from his mouth. "Wonderful! I'll let you know what I discover."

As they passed into the business area of town, Molly pointed out interesting signs, curious shops, and fascinating people. She spoke as if nothing were different between them.

Perhaps he thought too hard about this. If he took a step back, maybe he could see more clearly. With that in mind, Eli focused all of his attention on Molly and her musings.

"Look at that!" she said, pointing into the window of a store that sold toys for children. "Jasper had an entire army of little soldiers just like those when we were young. He used to leave them lying about the floors, and I was forever stepping on them and injuring my feet."

Eli grinned as he imagined a miniature version of Molly pouting over stepping on a tiny toy soldier. "I had the same ones."

"I'm certain you returned yours to their rightful places after playing with them, however," Molly said, glancing up at him.

"Oh, of course," Eli replied in his most serious tone.

"Hmm." She narrowed her eyes at him in a playful manner before leading the way to the next store window, which held a display of men's and women's hats.

"I'm well-stocked with hats," Eli said.

MOLLY 65

Molly drew her eyes from the window. "I've only ever seen you in that one." She nodded at the worn brown hat he wore. "You wore it to the dance, too."

"Like I said, I'm well-stocked with hats." He winked at her and she shook her head in mock exasperation as they moved on past the millinery.

"If you ever change your mind, Hill's General Store would be happy to order you a bowler or—" She paused when Eli stopped walking. "What is it?"

He nodded at the lumberyard on the corner just ahead. "That was my father's business." A new sign proudly proclaimed it sold "Denver's Finest Lumber" and that "Morton R. Adams, Jr." owned the business. "There used to be a large sign there with his name on it. See that building?" He pointed to a little shack that served as the office, unchanged from how he remembered it.

Molly nodded.

"My sisters and I used to play in there while Pa was out helping customers and Ma did the shopping." So many memories came with this lumberyard. "We'd play hide-and-seek after the sales closed for the day. Sometimes I'd trail after Pa, watching him show off the different sorts of wood to customers. He'd let me pretend to help him tally up the sales at the end of the day."

"Those sound like good memories." Her arm was still looped around his and she looked up at him with a kind smile.

"He wanted me to take over the business." He said the words tentatively. It still stung sometimes, his own guilt at not wanting the business his father created. But he knew, even when he was young, that it wasn't the life for him. He'd craved something different. Still, his father had hoped Eli might change his mind one day.

"Oh?" Molly studied his face a moment before glancing back at the lumberyard. "I must say, I can't picture you as a salesman. I believe you made the right decision."

Eli hadn't realized how badly he'd wanted to hear those words from her. Relief floated through him, and he smiled at her sweet face. She returned it, so genuine and open.

She tilted her head. "What's on your mind?"

What was always on his mind? He should tell her today. The thought made his stomach clench, but he needed to speak the words aloud. To have her hear them before she darted away from him yet again. Before she spent too much time with Emerson or Preston or any of those men who had more money than Eli could ever imagine.

Before he lost her forever.

Chapter Eleven

"WE'RE HALFWAY BACK to Cañon City by now," Eli said as Molly led him down yet another alley.

She shot him a mischievous grin. "I promise I know the way. If only a certain lawman would hush and follow my lead."

He dodged a puddle of mysterious origin—or perhaps not so mysterious considering a pile of horse dung lay nearby. "If anyone saw us back here, we'd be the talk of the town by nightfall."

Molly smiled to herself until she realized what she was doing. Since when did she not mind having her reputation ruined with Eli Jennings? Truth be told, she'd been having all sorts of thoughts about Eli lately, each one more confusing than the last.

"How do you know these alleys so well already? Please tell me we're getting closer," he said, grasping her hand to lead her away from yet another puddle.

Molly tried to pull her mind away from his strong grip on her hand to his actual question. "Yes, not much farther now. Look, you can see it from here." She pointed with her free hand at her aunt and uncle's house.

When they arrived, Eli led her around the small carriage house and barn and through the little garden that sat between the house and the outbuildings. He stopped just shy of the steps to the narrow porch where Aunt Ellen often enjoyed the evening air.

"Thank you for a lovely stroll," Molly said.

"I don't know that I'd call that last part a *stroll*." His hand still held hers, and her heart beat wildly as she wondered *why*. There were no puddles to steer her around, no obstacles in their path. They were standing still, outside the house, and yet he still loosely held her hand in his own.

"You enjoyed that little adventure," she said, tilting her chin up.

"I suppose I did. I should be the one thanking you for your assistance in my investigation."

"They'll all three be calling later this week."

Eli's hazel eyes darkened, the green disappearing into the brown, and he frowned.

"What is it?" Molly asked, although the second the words were out of her mouth, she wished she hadn't. Eli had closed his eyes as if he were in pain. He said nothing.

"Eli?" she whispered.

He opened his eyes again, regarding her as if she were something precious and breakable. "Molly, I . . ."

"Yes?" she prompted gently.

He looked down at their clasped hands like that might give him strength. "There's something I need to tell you."

"What is it?" she said again, beginning to wonder if it was something terrible. Was there something she needed to know about one of the men? Had he discovered something awful in his father's papers?

He looked up at her, hair falling from under that worn hat, that familiar tanned face appearing so concerned that she wanted to shake the information out of him. He gripped her hand a little tighter, and that was when the unthinkable occurred to her.

Was he jealous of her suitors?

The very idea nearly took her breath away. And yet it made her want to smile at the same time. Try as she might, she'd been able to summon no interest at all in the men who'd crowded around her at the dance. She wanted to say something that would appease Eli—if that was the root of the look she'd seen in his eyes just a moment ago. "I'll suffer the attentions of Mr. Preston, Mr. Edwards, and Mr. Emerson, only to gather the information you need."

And it was as if her words had lifted a weight from his mind. His entire face seemed to lighten with what she'd said and his grip on her hand eased.

Molly could've fallen over backwards with the knowledge she'd just gained. She felt as light as a feather, as if Eli's hand were the only thing anchoring her to earth. If he had feelings for her, why had he not acted on them in all of those months they'd known each other?

They stood there for a moment longer, before Eli finally cleared his throat. "I'll see you soon?"

She nodded, and before she knew it, he'd released her hand and was making his way back to the alley. She watched him go, and when he glanced back, she smiled and wondered how it was that she'd come all the way to Denver only to find herself falling for a man from Cañon City.

Chapter Twelve

RAIN PATTERED AGAINST the window of the study Saturday afternoon as Eli sorted through yet another stack of his father's papers. He'd been at it for days, finding little beyond the names of men and businesses Pa had worked with. Bills, receipts, purchase agreements, notes—Pa had kept everything.

Eli stood and took a sip of the coffee Ma had brought in earlier. The rain reminded him of that morning when Molly had been out with Paul Carter and had invited him out of the rain and into Carter's carriage. The memory made him smile at first, but then brought to mind the other men who sought Molly's attention. She'd just as much said she was uninterested in them after they returned from their walk into town, yet they had so much more to offer than Eli did. Those men had money and prestige. They could set Molly up in a beautiful home in Denver, and she'd want for nothing. Eli had a respectable job, certainly, but that was all. It made him happy, but was it enough to satisfy Molly?

If only he'd been able to get the words out that afternoon after their walk. He'd tried, but they'd lodged somewhere in his throat. Why was telling her how he felt so terrifying?

Eli returned to the desk chair and began sorting through the stack of papers again. His mind still half on Molly, he almost didn't hear the knock at the door.

It came more insistently and there was no mistaking it this time. Eli rose and went to the hallway, wondering who would come to the door in this weather. He pulled it open, and there, looking bedraggled despite the carriage on the street, stood Molly.

She smiled at him and he stood there blinking like a fool. Sense finally overcame him, and he opened the door wider so she could come inside.

"I'm sorry, I know this is highly unusual, and well . . . perhaps I should go?" Molly glanced back toward her carriage.

"No, it's quite all right. This scandal should have the entire neighborhood talking." Eli meant it as a joke, and after a second, Molly smiled. "I doubt anyone saw, given the rain. And besides, my mother is here. I'm certain it'll take her all of five minutes to be in the parlor to meet you." What he didn't put into words was the way his entire mood had lifted the second she'd shown up at his door. She risked her reputation to see him. Not Preston or any of those other men, but *him*.

Molly glanced around the tiny entry of their small home, and Eli had to bite his tongue to keep from apologizing for it. It was a perfectly nice home, but it was nothing compared to her aunt and uncle's house.

He took her wet coat and hung it from a peg near the fireplace in the parlor. Molly sat in one of the simple chairs nearby and laid her damp gloves on her lap. Eli took the seat that was angled next to hers. "Might I ask what I've done to deserve this visit?"

Molly's dark brown eyes lit up and she leaned forward. "I couldn't keep it to myself any longer. Mr. Emerson and Mr. Edwards called yesterday, and Mr. Preston came this morning.

They each spoke at length about their companies—it's so easy to get them to talk about business. And thankfully, they're all much more amusing and far less awful than, well, you know."

Eli pushed his lips together, trying hard not to think about any of those men spending time with Molly. Or what she meant by "amusing."

"But here is what I wanted to tell you. You may cross Mr. Edwards off your list. He informed me that his father is selling their business for an excellent price and packing up to move back East. He'd have no interest in collecting old debts. But both Mr. Preston and Mr. Emerson told me that extending loans was something they did regularly. The interest brings income to the business. Of course, neither would tell me who they lent money to, but they said they employed different tactics to collect payments when debtors didn't pay."

Eli inched forward in his chair. "What sort of tactics?"

"This is particularly interesting," she said. A drop of water inched its way from Molly's hair down her cheek, making it hard for Eli to concentrate on her words. Eli wanted to reach forward and brush it away with his thumb. He wondered what she'd do if he acted on that urge.

Molly reached up and swiped the drop away, staring at him intently. "Eli?"

"I'm sorry. Go on." His face warmed, and he hoped she'd attribute any redness to the heat of the fire.

"Of course they each said they sent letters to the debtors—"

"I've found no such letters."

"Perhaps your father threw them away."

That would be so unlike Pa. In fact, all of this was unlike the man Eli thought he knew. "What else?"

"If the debtor didn't pay then, they'd make a call. And then, if necessary, they'd pursue legal action."

"Make a call," Eli repeated. Was that what was happening? If so, it was only a matter of time before the man filed suit against Ma. If, of course, the debts truly existed.

"Yes," Molly said. "Of course, I have no way to tell if either of them would be so terrible as to invent debts that don't exist. They're both so nice, I can't imagine it, though."

The rain pattered steadily against the window as Eli tried to think through all that Molly had said. Her information helped, but it did nothing to narrow down the possibilities. For all Eli knew, the man paying his mother visits could be someone else entirely. He felt as if he were no closer at all to discovering the man's identity, even though he'd been searching for nearly three weeks.

And then, of course, nearly drowning out anything to do with his mother's predicament was Molly herself. And her pronouncement of Emerson and Preston as "nice." What did that mean?

"I rushed over here because I thought the information might be useful, but now I'm unsure," she said as she twisted her hands together in her lap.

"It's helpful." He smiled at her and reached across to still her hands. His heart hammered, and he hoped she wouldn't draw them away. She didn't a few days ago, when he'd held on much too long upon their return to the Blanchets' home.

Molly glanced down at his hand covering hers. It was as if time stilled, broken only by the rain tapping on the glass, and finally, she looked up at him. "I'm glad. I wish I could have learned more."

Eli drew in a breath, thinking of her spending more time with those men. "I'd rather you didn't."

Molly tilted her head. "How come? They might say something useful."

"It could be dangerous." Nothing about Preston or Emerson said *danger*, but it sounded better than *I don't want you to*.

"Dangerous?" A smile teased her lips up.

"Yes, very."

"Hmm . . ." She pursed her lips together, and Eli couldn't look away.

The rain pounded out a rhythm and he raised his other hand to trace the outline of her jaw. He didn't dare think too much about it, because if he did, he'd pull away immediately. But as it was, he lost all ability to think when she closed her eyes. "Molly."

She made a humming sound, and he stilled his hand, letting the palm cup her cheek. Her skin was softer than anything he'd ever touched.

"There is something I've been meaning to tell you."

She said nothing, and he knew he ought to say it now. The words built in his throat, but fell away when her lips parted just a little. He let his thumb drift down to touch the corner of them. She shivered, and that was all he needed. Keeping his hand on her cheek, he leaned forward. Their lips weren't even an inch apart, and his mind raced as fast as his heart. Molly was here, in front of him, and she wasn't pulling away. He didn't dare put feelings into words, not now. Not when it seemed she wanted him as much as he wanted her.

He could feel her soft breath against his lips. Just as he was about to press them to hers, a squeak sounded from the staircase.

Chapter Thirteen

COLD AIR ASSAULTED Molly's face as Eli dropped his hand and drew away faster than a horse from a snake.

"Eli?" a woman's voice called.

Molly twisted away, her face hot and her heart thumping. What had just happened? What was it that Eli had wanted to tell her?

"Ma." Eli stood, looking entirely composed. Only the slight pink tinge to his face gave away the fact that he'd almost kissed her.

Molly pressed a hand to her cheek and looked away from Eli's mother, who'd just entered the room. She willed the burning in her cheeks to fade and her pulse to slow. Slowly, she stood, just as Eli introduced her to his mother.

"Oh, Miss Hill! How wonderful to finally meet you." Eli's mother was a fair-haired, round woman who beamed at Molly.

"I'm pleased to meet you too," Molly said, forcing her voice to remain steady. What did she mean by *finally*?

"Eli said he had a friend who happened to be in Denver also," Mrs. Jennings said as she sat in the chair Eli had taken earlier.

A friend. A sick feeling invaded Molly's stomach. She glanced up at Eli, but he showed no emotion. Was that how he thought of her, just like every other man in Cañon City? Per-

MOLLY 77

haps what had just happened between them was nothing—just an accidental byproduct of Molly letting herself flirt with him. Enough of her friends at home had found themselves brokenhearted after similar incidents. Molly had heard enough stories to know that a man wanting to kiss her didn't necessarily mean he felt anything more for her. And yet, the way Eli had looked at her . . . She honestly thought he might. She wished his face would convey something—anything—to help her figure this out.

Eli's mother kept up most of the conversation. Molly snuck glances at Eli. Occasionally, he met her eyes, and a couple of times he gave her a smile. It was enough to bring the hope rushing back. It made her feel impulsive. An idea formed quickly.

"Mrs. Jennings, I'd love to invite the both of you to a dinner party at my aunt and uncle's home. This coming Friday." As she spoke, Molly grew even more excited about the idea. Aunt Ellen would be delighted; it was Uncle John who might need more convincing, but she was certain her aunt could wear him down.

"A dinner party? How lovely!" Mrs. Jennings's smile overtook her face even as Eli simply looked confused.

"We'll have some of the most prominent families in the city in attendance." At least she hoped they would, given the last-minute invitation. She rattled off a few names as she watched Eli's expression, hoping he might understand what she was offering him. His eyebrows seemed to disappear into his hair when she mentioned the Prestons and the Emersons. "May I count on your attending?"

"Of course! Thank you, dear. I'm sure it will be splendid!" Mrs. Jennings grabbed Eli's hand. "Won't it be, Eli?"

"Yes," he said a bit stiffly. "It will."

Molly drew her lower lip between her teeth. He was afraid of how he'd be received after the episode at the Prestons' dance. She gave him a confident smile.

It would be *her* dinner party, and she'd ensure no one made Eli feel uncomfortable under her family's roof.

MOLLY GLANCED ABOUT her aunt and uncle's long dining-room table. The table was full, and the dinner party was off to a wonderful start. Aunt Ellen had seemed to take it as a personal challenge to plan and execute such an event with only a few days' notice. Molly had thrown herself into helping. While she was happy that most of the guests they'd invited had accepted, she was particularly satisfied to see both Mr. Preston and Mr. Emerson in attendance. She'd only briefly had the opportunity to speak with Eli when he arrived with his mother. She hoped he would take advantage of the chance to speak with each of the men. She'd even strategically placed them nearby to make conversation easier.

Yet, as the dessert course was served, Eli, whom she'd seated across from her, conversed only with Miss Emilia Prentice, who sat to his left, and not with either Mr. Emerson or Mr. Preston, who sat on either side of Molly. It would be rude of him to ignore the ladies sitting on either side of him, but she'd assumed he'd chat with them only as long as propriety demanded before striking up conversation with the men.

Instead, she found herself fending off flirtatious conversation with each of the gentlemen. Thankfully, neither was as horrible as Mr. Browning or as dull as Mr. Carter. Molly kept a smile on her face as they vied for her attention and wished mightily Eli would look away from Miss Prentice.

As he laughed at something Emilia said, another thought occurred to Molly. Perhaps he didn't speak with anyone else because he was more interested in Emilia. Molly had made her acquaintance at the birthday celebration she'd attended, and Emilia and her mother had come calling soon after. Emilia was friendly, though a bit shy, and quite pretty, with strawberry blonde ringlets that framed her round face and perfectly shaped pink lips.

"Miss Hill?"

Molly jerked her attention away from Eli and Emilia. Mr. Preston was looking at her, waiting for her response to a question she hadn't heard. "Pardon?"

"I'd wondered if you might enjoy an excursion to the opera? Forrester's Opera House is getting up a new production next week." The gas lights in the dining room shone off Mr. Preston's head as he smiled at her.

"Oh, I—"

"Perhaps you prefer the theater?" Mr. Emerson cut in. "I find the theater more interesting than the opera."

"Well—"

"More *interesting*?" Mr. Preston let out a short, nervous laugh.

Molly sighed as the two bickered over the theater and the opera, and her attention wandered back to Eli. She wished she could toss her napkin at him. That would get his attention. He was wasting precious time, sharing smiles with Emilia when he could be speaking with these men instead. The men who were now bothering her, when in fact, she would enjoy neither the theater nor the opera. She much preferred walks out of doors or small gatherings of friends. Eli knew this, considering they'd discussed a traveling theatrical group when it came to Cañon City early last fall.

She frowned at Eli as Emilia laughed at something he'd said. Perhaps she *would* pitch her napkin at him. It would serve him right. Not only was he wasting time, he'd nearly kissed her a few days ago. Who would do such a thing and then flirt with another lady? Unless . . .

Molly's doubts had been spot-on. She *was* just a friend to him. He'd gotten confused with her acting otherwise, and now he regretted it.

She realized, her heart sinking, that she was absolutely right.

Chapter Fourteen

SMOKE DRIFTED TO THE ceiling in the dining room after the ladies had adjourned to the drawing room. Eli sat back in his chair, the conversation of the other men moving around him like the smoke. The dinner had been a long, drawn-out, torturous affair. He'd spent the entire meal vainly trying not to stare at Molly. She was so beautiful tonight, with her dark hair looking softer than velvet and a shimmering white and gold dress that seemed to make her glow. And he clearly wasn't the only one who'd noticed—Emerson and Preston hadn't looked away from her all night. Watching the two of them fall all over themselves to claim her attention only served to rouse a primal desire to shove them both out of the way, and so Eli had kept his attention on the friendly Miss Prentice instead.

But now, with Molly off in the drawing room, he felt as if he could breathe again. Emerson was regaling the others with a story involving a saloon and—Eli thought he'd heard—a monkey.

"And then the fellow said no, so I socked him in the stomach. The monkey disappeared off into the streets. No one's seen hide nor hair of him since." Emerson finished with a flourish of his cigar.

The men around them laughed, and conversation turned to various instances of fisticuffs.

"I'd bet you it wasn't anything like the way Jennings here punched Browning in the face," a man whose name had escaped Eli said in response to another man's claim.

Eli shifted in his seat as the others' attention turned to him. Preston, he noticed, was the only one not smiling. Not surprising, since it was his family's affair Eli had interrupted.

"That wasn't anything," he said, trying to shrug it off. He wished they'd speak of something else. Ideally, something to do with business so he could suss out more information from Preston and Emerson. He'd barely gotten anywhere with either of them.

"Wasn't anything," the man who'd first spoken said with a laugh. "The man wore a black eye all week."

The others murmured in agreement as Preston glared at Eli.

Eli shrugged. "Can't believe no one's seen that monkey," he said in the hopes of shifting the conversation.

"Why'd you hit him?" Preston asked as the room went silent.

Eli pondered for a moment how to answer without besmirching Molly's reputation or saying anything he'd regret about Browning, as much as the man might deserve it. "He made Miss Hill uncomfortable."

Preston frowned while Emerson looked downright angry. As much as Eli couldn't stand either one of them spending time with Molly, at least these two seemed to be decent men. Which made it harder to believe either of them was the one responsible for demanding money from Eli's mother.

"I'm glad you saw it," Emerson said, as the older men near them engaged in a discussion of local politics.

"I am too," Eli replied. He didn't want to think about what might have happened if he hadn't stepped in. His actions might have made him persona non grata at some of the men's homes, but that was nothing at all compared to Molly's safety.

"She's a sweet girl," Preston said as he raised a water glass to his mouth.

"That she is." Emerson's voice was polite but Eli detected a slight edge to it.

Eli said nothing at all, despite the almost overwhelming desire to claim Molly as his in front of both these men. Annoying them would get him nowhere with his investigation.

Preston cast a glance at Emerson before saying, "She gave me a little token of her affection just the other day."

His meaning was clear yet covert enough not to be construed as ungentlemanly, particularly as he looked at Emerson with a smug smile. He'd implied Molly had kissed him. Emerson pressed his lips into a line, but that was nothing compared to what raged inside Eli.

Eli clenched his hands into fists under the table as rising flames inside tempted him to fire back at Preston. He wouldn't though. The brief moments he'd shared with Molly—the ones in which he'd very nearly kissed her—were theirs alone, and none of the business of any of the men seated at this table.

Unless it was also something she'd shared with Preston.

Eli stared at the man, as if that would make the truth evident. He wouldn't believe it. He *couldn't* believe Molly was the sort of girl who went about kissing every man who called on her. She'd just as much as said she had no interest in Preston or Emerson . . . hadn't she? Preston was exaggerating in an attempt to eliminate his competition, that was all.

It had to be. Eli's heart couldn't stand for it to be otherwise.

Chapter Fifteen

MOLLY EMERGED FROM Mr. Preston's Brougham carriage with a sigh of relief. He was nice enough, she mused as she allowed him to escort her to the door, but nothing about him made her heart beat faster. She didn't yearn to see him again or wish he'd take her hand. Even with his balding pate, he wasn't unattractive with his dark blue eyes and kind smile, but he simply was not the man for her. Even worse, every moment she spent in his company, she kept finding herself unintentionally comparing him to Eli.

"Thank you for a lovely drive," she said, quickly extricating her arm from his at the door.

He reached for her hand, but she deftly maneuvered it to adjust her hat. He raised his awkwardly to smooth down the side of his hair. "I enjoyed it too. I'll call on you again next week, if that's suitable?"

Molly cringed inside, but forced herself to nod. She had to help Eli discover if Mr. Preston was the one to whom his father owed a debt, although she couldn't imagine him threatening Mrs. Jennings. Mr. Preston was simply too *nice*.

She reached for the doorknob just as he tried again to claim her hand. "Goodbye, Mr. Preston. I'll see you soon." She smiled at him as she slipped inside and then shut the door, leaving him looking a bit bereft on the front porch.

Inside, she leaned against the doors. This was getting much harder. The more time she spent with Mr. Preston and Mr. Emerson, the more they believed she was interested in them. And the more they believed that, the worse she felt. It was wrong to lead them on so, and yet she could discover things Eli couldn't.

One more visit with each of them, she told herself. She'd have to find out then, even if she had to ask very pointed questions. She couldn't push it any farther and continue to feel like a decent person.

Besides, she wished to spend her time with someone else.

It was strange, thinking of Eli in that way, and yet it felt right. Of course, that nagging doubt that he didn't feel the same way about her still sat in her stomach like a swallowed cherry pit. Molly pushed away from the door and removed her wrap. The afternoons had finally grown warm enough that she thought she might be able to leave it behind. Stevens the butler appeared from seemingly nowhere and took the wrap from her, along with her reticule.

"Mr. Jennings awaits in the parlor," Stevens said with a pained voice. "I informed him you were out, and yet he insisted on waiting."

"Thank you, Stevens," Molly said. She gave him a smile to let him know it was all right—in fact, it was more than all right given the way her stomach seemed to flutter—and yet the butler's expression remained the same.

In the parlor, Eli stood before the cold fireplace. He looked up when she entered, a smile immediately alighting upon his face. The fact that he looked so happy to see her made her feel giddy. She paused and gripped the doorframe, lest she find herself running into his arms or acting in some other foolish way. "Good afternoon, Eli. What brings you here?"

"I became curious about what else you might have discovered." He shoved his hands into the pockets of his trousers.

"Curious enough you waited . . . how long for my return?" She oughtn't push him, and yet seeing him grow flustered was just the reward for which she'd hoped. Perhaps the attention he'd paid Emilia at the dinner party meant nothing.

"It wasn't long," he said quickly. "Stevens—you know, I don't believe he much cares for me—said you were out with Mr. Preston, and so I decided to wait." His jaw worked as he looked at her. "To see what you learned, of course."

"Of course." Molly bit her bottom lip to keep from smiling. She let go of the doorframe and entered the room. Her aunt was out making calls herself, or she might have talked Eli's ear off for however long he'd been here.

She glanced at the settee, thinking she should offer him a seat, and yet she didn't feel as if she could sit herself. A restless energy moved through her, and she gripped her hands together to try to calm it.

Eli stood immediately in front of her, just a few inches away, and she was conscious of every single one of those inches. She found her voice buried somewhere deep down inside her. "I fear I didn't learn much from Mr. Preston today. He did mention losing money on some investments, but he seemed optimistic about recovering the lost funds."

Eli frowned. "He likely made it seem less serious than it is."

"But why would he do that?"

His frown turned into something flat and emotionless. "The last thing he wants is his prospective wife thinking his business is in trouble."

His prospective wife. Molly wanted to laugh at the words, but she couldn't. It was just the thing she'd feared standing in the entry a few minutes ago. All the more reason to wrap this up as quickly as possible. She had no desire at all to become Mrs. Preston.

"I wish you'd been able to talk with him more at the dinner party," she said, brushing those thoughts aside. "Perhaps I shouldn't have sat you beside Miss Prentice." She meant for the last sentence to come out lightly and teasing, but a pained expression shot across Eli's face before disappearing into something more stiff. It was a look that made her feel as if the sheriff's deputy were standing in her parlor, and not the Eli she'd come to know over the past several months.

"It simply wasn't the right opportunity," he said, his voice as empty as his expression.

Whatever in the world was wrong with him? She took a step forward, hoping to tease out a smile or a twinkle in his eye. "I could wrangle you an invitation to the Taylors' dinner party next weekend. Or there's the church social. You wouldn't need an invitation to attend that." She smiled up at him as she imagined the two of them sharing a slice of cake.

"No, that's quite all right, thank you," he said, finally extricating his hands from his pockets. Molly wished one of them would find her hand and draw her forward. And yet, he made no such move, instead resting one hand on the back of the wing chair while letting the other hang at his side.

Something felt off, and yet Molly couldn't pinpoint it. *Was it Miss Prentice?* It couldn't be. They barely knew each other. And if he desired to know her better, he'd be jumping at the opportunity to attend another social event.

She twisted her hands together and searched for something to say. "Mr. Emerson is coming around tomorrow. I'll let you know what I discover."

Eli let out a breath and moved toward the fireplace. He stopped, facing the mantel, his eyes on something Molly couldn't discern. "You needn't do so. I'll find a way to meet with him."

"It's fine. I don't mind," she said. "Would you like to sit?" She gestured at the chairs despite the fact he wasn't looking at her.

He turned abruptly, facing her again. "I ought to get home."

"All right." Molly tried to ignore the sinking feeling in her stomach. "Thank you for paying me a visit. I wish I had more information for you."

That same expression—the one that looked as if he'd chewed nails—crossed Eli's face. His jaw worked and for a moment Molly thought he had something he wanted to say. But whatever it was, he must have changed his mind. He crossed the room and she followed him.

In the hallway, she retrieved his hat. When he took it from her, his fingers lingered on hers for a moment. Molly drew in her breath as he caught her eyes, and hope ignited in her heart.

It lasted a brief moment. He gave her a smile, and all felt as it should again. Perhaps this situation with his mother had been weighing heavily on his mind, particularly since they hadn't uncovered anything useful lately. She mentally chastised herself for reading too much into his expressions and actions.

At the door, he took her hand. "I'll see you soon."

"Yes," she said. "Please give your mother my regards."

He smiled again, although there was something wistful about it. He bid her farewell, and as she watched him descend the stairs, she resolved to learn something useful from Mr. Emerson.

She'd do anything to relieve Eli of what worried him.

Chapter Sixteen

THE EVENING AIR WAS warm, and Eli was glad he hadn't hired a ride to Molly's aunt and uncle's house. He felt restless and frustrated, and this walk to the horse railroad stop was exactly what he needed.

The prospect of seeing her had driven him all day. While he sorted through more of his father's papers, he imagined her brown eyes meeting his. When he went out to pick up an order from the dry goods store for Ma, he pictured Molly's cheerful grin as they perused the store windows last week. And when he sent off a letter to Ben, all he could think about was how much he wished Ma hadn't interrupted them in the parlor. If she hadn't, he might have kissed Molly. And if he had . . .

He dodged a peddler who had set up shop on the boardwalk close to town. She'd been so eager to help him get to the bottom of this debt business that he hadn't thought about what might happen. And what had happened was Molly spending more time with men like Emerson and Preston. And the closer Eli got to her, the more it bothered him. There was the way she'd deftly kept up conversation with both men seated beside her at the dinner party, not once dropping her smile or sparing more than the occasional glance toward Eli. Then of course, there was Preston bragging about receiving a "token" of Molly's affection. Eli had just about convinced himself the man had said that only to get a leg up on Emerson, but then Molly said nothing when he'd referred to her as Preston's prospective wife.

His jaw clenched. Why didn't she say anything? He'd expected her to brush it off, to laugh at his words, *something*. But she hadn't. Did that mean the idea wasn't so far-fetched? And if it wasn't, why had she let Eli take her hands and almost kiss her?

Was she toying with him?

The thought stopped him dead in his tracks, and another gentleman nearly collided with him. "Pardon," Eli said as the man went around him, muttering. He started forward again, slower, as he pondered the thought he'd had.

She couldn't be. That wouldn't be like Molly at all. The Molly he knew was kind and honest. She wouldn't act one way when she felt another. But . . . wasn't that exactly what they'd decided she would do with her suitors?

Eli clenched his hands as he wound around people making their way into town. He'd set himself up for this. She'd suggested the idea, and he'd agreed. He let her become dishonest. And now he was paying for it.

The thoughts only made him angrier at himself. He'd been struggling so long with the idea that he needed to tell her how he felt, and yet he hadn't. If he'd been honest with her, maybe he wouldn't be in this situation. Maybe she wouldn't have needed to find men like Preston to court her.

If she felt the same way about him . . .

His mind spun as he found a seat on the horsecar. The same thoughts played over and over when he debarked and strode past shops and homes far less elegant than the Blanchets'. He was a few houses away from Ma's when he noticed the carriage.

It was another Brougham, black and nondescript and one of what seemed like hundreds in Denver, and it was parked on the street directly in front of Ma's house. It was late for callers, but perhaps a good friend had come to visit her.

But just as he'd decided that was the case, a man swept out the front door and headed straight for the carriage. A coat flew out behind him as he walked, despite the fact that it was too warm for a coat.

Eli narrowed his eyes. Could this be the man who'd been bothering his mother for repayment? He walked faster, and as the man drew closer to the carriage, Eli broke out into a run.

The driver opened the door and the man entered. The driver returned to his seat as Eli's feet pounded the wooden planks.

"Hold up!" he shouted. But if the driver heard him, he made no indication. Instead, he took up the lines and nudged the horse into action.

Eli drew up just past Ma's house as the carriage disappeared around the corner. His breath came quickly as he tried to remember as many details as possible about the man's conveyance. But there wasn't much to remember at all. It looked exactly like half the carriages in the city.

Frustrated for the second time that day, he bounded up the steps to Ma's house. He found her just inside, seated in the parlor, her eyes red and shiny.

"Ma?" Eli tossed his hat aside and went to her immediately. "Was that him? The man who's been demanding money?"

She nodded and clenched his arms. "He insists I pay him more by the end of the week or he'll have proceedings begun to take my house."

A growl sat low in Eli's throat as he consoled his mother. While he didn't know who the visitor was, he knew without a doubt the man was a coward, coming here while Eli was gone. And that fact made it even more likely the debt was fabricated. The man knew Eli wouldn't be as good a target as his widowed mother.

"I'll fix this," he said to Ma.

And he would, if it was the last thing he did.

Chapter Seventeen

MOLLY CLAPPED A HAND to the pretty white napkin to keep the breeze from whisking it away, but she was too late. Mr. Emerson caught it easily as it skipped across his lap.

"Thank you," she said, smiling politely as he handed it back to her.

Since it was such a beautiful day, the church social was being held outdoors in the lot behind the church. It was a busy affair—people still lined up for plates of fried chicken, cold ham, and more side dishes than Molly had ever seen in one place. Even Aunt Ellen, who usually left the cooking to Mrs. Wheatley and her daughter at home, had made a colorful bean salad.

Mr. Emerson had spotted Molly the moment she arrived with her aunt and uncle. She'd hurriedly glanced about the attendees, hoping against hope that Eli had decided to come, but he was nowhere to be seen. In fact, she hadn't heard a word from him since he called on her several days ago.

Molly had tried not to dwell on how strangely he'd acted then. She ought to be glad Mr. Emerson was here and had sought her out so quickly. After all, if she could gather some more information from him, she could relay it to Eli and—hopefully—assuage the worry he carried that made him act so unlike himself.

"Do you care for more ham?" Mr. Emerson asked now.

"Oh no, I'm quite all right, thank you." Molly set her plate in her lap. Mr. Emerson hadn't been shy about filling it. If Molly ate anything more, she'd burst the laces on her corset. She searched her memory for something he'd told her about his family's hardware business. "Did you receive your shipment from St. Louis?"

His face lit up at her question. He really was a good man—kind and thoughtful, hardworking, and attentive. He just wasn't the man for Molly. It made a guilt rise inside her. She was using him to find out what she needed to share with Eli. She hadn't thought too much on it before, back when she barely knew Mr. Emerson or Mr. Preston. But the more time she'd spent with each of them, the worse she felt. She had no feelings of love or attraction for either of them. She wanted so badly to help Eli, but the distaste at *how* she was helping sat at the back of her throat. She needed to get this over with so she could gently let them both go.

"It arrived yesterday. Just in time, too, considering how many orders we needed to fill. We've been very busy lately." The Emersons had opened a hardware business just at the start of the building boom in Denver, and had profited well from their good timing. And according to Mr. Emerson, his father had invested their earnings wisely.

"That's wonderful," Molly replied. "Good fortune allows us to be generous with those who have less."

Mr. Emerson dabbed at the corner of his mouth with his napkin as he looked thoughtful. "You're right. I wonder how we might help?"

"Perhaps you could forgive some debts? Or donate to the new orphans' home," she added hurriedly.

Although it wasn't quick enough, because Mr. Emerson set his napkin down on the arm of his chair and tilted his head. "I can't help but notice your concern for debtors. I don't believe the Blanchets have purchased on credit, if that's your concern."

Molly's cheeks went pink. She wasn't as wily as she'd thought with these questions. "Oh, no, it isn't that. It's only . . . well, it's in the Scriptures, isn't it? 'Forgive us our debts, as we have forgiven our debtors.'"

"Yes," Mr. Emerson said, picking up a forkful of Aunt Ellen's bean salad. "It is, and it's what Reverend Hutton preached on a couple of weeks ago. It must have made quite the impression on you."

"It did," Molly agreed. She glanced about the crowd behind the church again, searching for one familiar face. People sat and stood as they ate, and behind them, the bustle of the town moved along, albeit a bit slower on a Sunday afternoon.

"Well, I'd have to speak with our accountant about that. I don't know much about who owes what to the company. But perhaps we can make that happen."

Molly bestowed a smile upon him, even as she felt she were no closer to discovering the truth. Although she highly doubted Mr. Emerson was the man visiting Eli's mother. But still, that didn't eliminate anyone else who worked for his business. It could be the accountant, it could be Mr. Emerson's father or his younger brother. For all Molly knew, it could be the man who cleaned the floors.

Perhaps this entire ruse had been nothing but futile. Neither Mr. Emerson nor Mr. Preston kept the accounts at their respective companies. And if that was true, what was she doing, then?

"Molly—I hope it's all right I call you that?" Mr. Emerson had set his empty plate on the ground and was now looking at her intently.

"I . . ." Molly trailed off, completely flustered by the thoughts she'd been having and by his question. She needed to tell Eli this wasn't working. And then she needed to let Mr. Emerson and Mr. Preston go before she wound up hurting them.

Mr. Emerson must have taken her confusion for something else, because he reached for both of her hands. "Molly, you are the most beautiful girl I've ever known, and the smartest too. If it's all right with you, I'd like to speak with your uncle about courting you. Would you like that?"

Molly blinked at him. Courting? Was that not what he was already doing? Molly wouldn't know—after all, no man had ever courted her before. It was strange, how badly she'd wanted a handsome, smart, kind man to do just this—and now she didn't want it at all. At least, not from Mr. Emerson. What should she say? If she told him no, right here in front of the entire church, how would he take it? But she couldn't say yes, not when her heart was . . .

Not when her heart was with Eli.

"Miss Hill? Might I steal a moment of your time?" a male voice, the edges rough with barely contained emotion, said from just nearby.

Molly jerked her head up as she pulled her hands away from Mr. Emerson.

Eli looked down at her, his face a storm on the horizon.

Chapter Eighteen

"NOW SEE HERE, WE WERE having a conversation." Emerson rose from his seat, his hands balled into fists.

Eli tightened his jaw. If the man wanted trouble, he'd give him trouble—even if they were at a church social. "I must speak with Miss Hill immediately."

"Miss Hill is—"

"Gentlemen, please." Molly pushed her way between them. "Mr. Emerson, let me speak with Mr. Jennings. It'll be just a moment."

The look of surprise Emerson gave Molly quickly disappeared into sheer anger when he turned back to Eli. Eli returned that look with a tight smile before turning and striding away, Molly on his heels.

"What are you doing?" she demanded when he stopped at the edge of the crowd near the street. "Are you trying to start a fight?"

He crossed his arms, hoping that might contain the ugliness rising inside him. The thoughts he'd been having all week that had continued to grow the more they weighed on his mind threatened now to burst out of him like water from a dam. "What were *you* doing? I thought you were gathering information, but instead you were ... you were ..." He gestured with a hand when the words wouldn't come.

"I was *what* exactly? Please, Eli, enlighten me." Molly's arms were drawn against her sides, and her face was the very image of polite fury. She'd never looked at him like that before. In fact, he'd never seen her look at *anyone* like that before.

"You looked awfully cozy." The image of her allowing Emerson to hold her hands—the hands *he'd* held—ate at his very core.

"What do you expect me to do, push him away? Where would that leave your mother?" Molly took a deep breath as she glared at him. "Before you interrupted like a boor, I was going to tell you that I don't think this is very useful."

Eli raised his eyebrows. "And yet you continued with it?"

Molly pressed her lips together before huffing loudly and throwing her hands up. "You are insufferable, Eli Jennings. I don't know what you want from me."

I want you. The thought clawed at his insides, begging to be released, but he clamped his mouth shut. He'd not tell her here, where she could reject him in front of what felt like half of Denver.

"At least I know where Mr. Emerson stands," she said.

Her words hurtled into him, their impact causing him to suck in a breath. "What does that mean?"

She straightened, pushing her shoulders back. "I believe you know exactly what it means. Enjoy the social, Eli." And with that, she turned and strode back toward where Emerson sat.

Eli stood in place, anger warring with jealousy as sadness crept in around the edges. What had he done?

No. She understood how he felt, even if he couldn't put it into words. She'd just as much as said so, and yet she chose Emerson over him.

Eli stalked away, leaving the happy chatter and the scent of fried chicken behind him. He shuttered his heart with every angry thought he could muster.

He'd come to Denver for one reason, and it was high time he put all his attention to that matter. He'd deal with his heart—and his feelings for the woman he'd just left behind—later.

Chapter Nineteen

TWO DAYS AFTER THE church social, Molly drifted about her room like a ghost. Mr. Preston had come calling earlier, and she'd feigned a headache after ten minutes. Aunt Ellen had sent her to bed, but Molly found it impossible to lie still. Thoughts tumbled through her head, disjointed and useless.

She wandered to the window in her room, which overlooked the street below. One thing was absolutely clear, and that was she could not get Eli out of her thoughts. She'd believed they had something—almost dared to think that she was falling in love with him—but he'd changed.

She'd thought he was worried over his mother's situation, but it was clear at the social that he was jealous. He didn't trust her, and she couldn't abide that. How many times had Mama mentioned that trust was the foundation of a long-lasting marriage? If Eli couldn't believe she felt nothing for Mr. Emerson or Mr. Preston, how would he believe her if she confessed her feelings to him? After all, he'd agreed to this scheme. He knew she'd have to spend time with these men in order to gather information. If she pushed them away, how could she learn more?

And then, of course, there was the guilt. That had grown steadily since she'd put a name to it at the church social. When Mr. Preston had arrived this morning, his eager smile had made her feel terrible. Both he and Mr. Emerson had feelings for her. That was clear as day.

Molly smiled wryly at the window. She'd thought Eli had feelings for her too. He'd had the opportunity to voice them, but he never did. Instead, he'd become angry and distrustful. Why, upon seeing Mr. Emerson with her, hadn't he confessed his own feelings instead of acting like a jealous schoolboy? Why hadn't he asked to court her, as Mr. Emerson had? If he truly loved her, he would have already asked. He would have put a stop to this investigation a long time ago.

No matter what, she was ending this nonsense. She'd uncovered nothing helpful, and all she'd managed to do was put the feelings of two very nice men into jeopardy.

A hansom cab rolled by on the street below, and it seemed to draw the curtain away from Molly's eyes. She'd come to Denver to find love and an opportunity for marriage. She would let Mr. Preston and Mr. Emerson down as kindly as she could, she'd try to forget Eli, and she'd look again among the men of Denver.

While the resolution cleared her head, it did nothing for the heaviness in her heart. And Molly feared Eli would occupy that part of her forever.

Chapter Twenty

ELI CLUTCHED THE SMALL ivory sheet of paper in his hand as he made his way toward Emerson's Hardware Company. He'd found it late last night, when he went through the last of his father's papers. Sleep was impossible, considering each time he lay down, all he could think of was Molly. So instead, he'd thrown himself into paperwork, and this time, it had paid off.

The little sheet of paper indicated that Pa had purchased a variety of tools from Emerson's company on credit, just one month before his death. The final amount wasn't much by any means, but Eli had found nothing that indicated the debt had been paid. Likely, Pa had passed on before it was. The lawyer for Pa's estate ought to have settled it through the sale of the business, and yet Eli had found nothing in the estate documents that showed payment.

He was almost certain Emerson—or someone working for him—was the man paying visits to Eli's mother. And yet the amount owed was far less than what she'd paid the man who called himself Smith so far. That was what made no sense. Either Eli was wrong, or Emerson was using this debt as an excuse to extract more money from Ma.

That thought drove him forward, until he stood in front of the hardware store, which spanned nearly half a block with its shop and offices. The Emersons had done very well with this business. And yet if they had, why was George Emerson extorting money from Eli's mother?

Eli shook his head and moved toward the door, when he realized the place was closed for the evening. He should have come earlier, instead of spending so much time debating the best way forward and then wasting time with the police, who'd told him he didn't have enough proof to pursue the matter. He sighed and turned toward the street.

A carriage rattled by—a very familiar carriage. Eli drew in a breath. Just inside, he could make out Molly. She didn't see him. She was focused instead on talking with her aunt who sat across from her. The carriage quickly passed him, leaving him with only the briefest memory of her beautiful hair, her smile, and eyes that seemed to speak her feelings.

Eli leaned against the building as regret inched its way into his consciousness. He'd had so much just a few days ago, and now it was gone. *But did you, though?* That tired jealousy still sat in the corners of his mind, yet it had lessened as the days had passed since the church social. And he feared Molly was absolutely right.

He had agreed she would try to get information from her suitors. He knew what that would cost him in his own feelings toward her. And yet, even as she spent more time with them, she also spent more time with *him*. Had he imagined the way she'd regarded him as if he were the only man alive? Had he made up the easy way she'd laughed at his jokes and listened so attentively when he spoke of his father? And perhaps he'd conjured up the way she seemed to want him to kiss her that day in his mother's parlor.

But every moment she'd spent with Emerson, or Preston, or any of those men had chipped away at the little confidence he had. And then when he saw Emerson's hands on hers, that confidence had sailed away entirely, an iceberg adrift in freezing waters, leaving only a shattered heart and the desire to lash out.

He wanted so badly to speak with her. To apologize. And—even if it killed him—to finally get the words out so she'd know without a doubt how he felt about her. But how?

Eli pushed away from the building and turned to contemplate it, if only to set aside the confusing thoughts about Molly. Perhaps the answer to who had been harassing his mother was just inside. He eyed the door. It wouldn't take much to force his way in.

He removed his hat and ran a hand through his hair. No, he wouldn't stoop to that. He was a lawman after all, and he had a duty to uphold.

Eli replaced his hat and determined to find Emerson on his own.

IT WAS NEARING TEN o'clock, and Eli had yet to lay eyes on Emerson. Molly had mentioned the man liked a game of cards now and then, and Eli had hoped this was one of those times. As he pushed open the door to the Silver Door Saloon—his third stop of the night—it wasn't lost on him that at least some of what Molly had collected was useful. He shoved that irritating thought down as he scanned the crowded room for Emerson.

And there he was, sprawled out on a chair at a table with four other men, all with cards in their hands. Eli narrowed his eyes through the haze of smoke that hung over the room. He hadn't thought through what he'd say if he actually found Emerson, but that didn't stop his feet from moving forward. He wove through men in various states of inebriation, women of uncertain character, and the chairs and tables that were strewn haphazardly through the saloon. Somewhere off to the left, a piano man banged out a raucous medley as people shouted and talked and laughed over it.

"George Emerson."

The men at the table all looked up at him. An older fellow laid a card down slowly but didn't take his eyes from Eli. Emerson took his time turning around in his chair. He looked Eli up and down with a confused smile. "You want in the game?"

"I don't gamble."

"All right," Emerson said as if he'd never heard of such a thing. He turned back to the other men at the table. "Jennings here is a lawman down in . . . Where is it you're from again? Colorado City?"

"Cañon City."

Emerson laid his cards facedown on the table as he stood. "Throw in some coins and play a little. These gentlemen won't take you for too much," he said with a grin at his friends. When Eli declined a second time, Emerson stood and clapped him on the back. "Come on, I'll buy you a drink."

The man's friendliness almost made Eli second-guess what he was doing here. Until he remembered the note he'd found just this morning among his father's papers. And, of course, Emerson's hands on Molly's and the way he'd looked into her eyes. Eli clenched his fists.

"I need to discuss something with you," he said.

Emerson raised his eyebrows. "All right. I'll fold, gentlemen." He didn't wait for Eli as he made his way to the scuffed wooden bar at the rear of the room and ordered two whiskeys. Eli stood next to him, not bothering to take a seat. Emerson pushed one glass toward Eli as he lifted the other. He downed the entirety of its contents before leaning against the bar. His dark hair fell into his very blue eyes, and by his easy grin, Eli guessed this wasn't the man's first whiskey of the night.

"Your company did business with my father," Eli said.

Emerson shrugged before signaling to the bartender for another drink. "On a regular basis, yes."

Eli wrapped a hand around his glass but didn't raise it. The last thing he needed right now was whiskey clouding his thoughts. They were murky enough as it was. "He purchased a large quantity of tools about a month before his death, on credit."

"That wasn't unusual," Emerson said. He nodded at the bartender who delivered another glass of amber-colored whiskey.

"I've found no evidence that he repaid that debt."

"I imagine it came from the estate after his death." Emerson finished his drink and set the glass on the bar. "I'm sorry for his passing."

"Thank you." Eli watched the man carefully. Was he feigning indifference? Or did he truly not know whether the debt existed? The only way to know was to ask him, but he had to do it carefully. "You see, I've been going through my family's papers—tying up loose ends—and it seems my mother has been paying off some of my pa's old debts."

Emerson's attention had wandered off somewhere across the saloon. Eli drew in a breath. He was being too careful, too vague. Time for something more direct. "A man calling himself Smith has been paying visits to my mother, for purposes of collecting debts. My mother has paid in full, and yet the man has increased the amount owed. He claims to be acting on your company's behalf."

That got Emerson's attention. His eyes—slightly bloodshot from the whiskey—snapped back to Eli. "What are you implying?"

Eli stood straighter, one hand resting on his gun belt. "Is your company extorting money from my mother?"

Emerson laughed. When Eli didn't join him, his laughter died into a frown. "I won't deign to answer that question. But I don't take kindly to smears on my reputation."

"Then why won't you answer the question?"

Emerson stiffened. Eli held his ground, waiting for the man's response. His fingers twitched and he curled them into fists.

Emerson glanced down and then drew his gaze back up to Eli's face. "Are you going to hit me like you did Browning?" When Eli didn't reply, he added, "Do it and you'll turn every man in this place against you. They all know me. They know my family. You'll find yourself sitting in jail if they don't teach you a lesson first."

Fire roared up Eli's insides. All he could think of was this dog touching Molly, smiling at her, charming her. His jaw worked as he fought to keep himself in check. Emerson wasn't worth it. "If it is you, I'll find out." And with that, he strode through the saloon and out the doors.

Outside, he sucked in great breaths of air as men went in and out of the saloon beside him. Emerson was a wolf in sheep's clothing. That friendly persona he wore in daylight was a mask. Eli wanted to lay the man out right there in the middle of the saloon, not only for what he'd done to Ma but also for the way he'd charmed Molly.

Molly... A manic laugh rose in the back of Eli's throat, but he stuffed it down and headed for home. Here he was, ready to start a fight he couldn't win, despite the fact that he'd just as much as accused her of allowing Emerson to take far too many liberties. But Emerson had deceived her, convincing her that he was a good man—and that infuriated Eli. What was it she'd said? "At least I know where Mr. Emerson stands." But she didn't... did she?

Eli stopped in the middle of the wooden walkway, the moon shining above. What she'd said had nothing to do with Emerson's character. He knew that the moment she'd said it, and he'd buried those words under layers of hurt and jealousy. Emerson had told her how he felt about her. And Eli hadn't.

Eli closed his eyes. He'd failed. After everything—after those moments they'd shared, the way he'd held her hand, how she would have let him kiss her if they hadn't been interrupted—he'd thrown it all away because he couldn't summon the courage to put his feelings into words.

She thought he didn't care.

But he did. So much that he couldn't imagine returning to Cañon City without her. He couldn't fathom not seeing her each day at the general store. He couldn't comprehend that she'd marry someone else, here in Denver.

Eli's eyes flew open.

He wouldn't let it happen. If he could confront Emerson with no qualms at all, he could speak plainly to Molly. He'd apologize for the jealousy he'd let get the best of him. And if she turned him down, so be it. At least he could return home with the knowledge that he'd done his best.

Eli walked toward Ma's house with new purpose. First thing tomorrow morning, he'd be at the Blanchets' door.

And he'd tell Molly the truth.

Chapter Twenty-one

THE SUN HAD BARELY crested the horizon when Molly awoke. She sat straight up in bed, the dream she'd had still vivid in her mind. She'd been at home in Cañon City. No, not the home she'd shared with her mother. Molly squeezed her eyes shut as her heart pounded. It was a different house, smaller and brand new, on the edge of town. She was holding a baby and waiting on the front steps for . . .

Eli.

Molly fell back into bed and drew the quilt over her eyes. She'd dreamed she was married to Eli. The cruel, false memories of the dream pricked at her heart. Molly pressed the quilt into her eyes to push away the tears that threatened. The resolution she'd made to herself just a few days earlier rang hollow. The truth was, she had no interest in the men of Denver.

Her only thoughts lay with the man who'd made it clear he didn't care enough for her to trust her. Try as she might, Molly couldn't reconcile that side of Eli with the man she'd known before. She'd fallen in love, that much was clear, but she'd fallen for the kind, thoughtful man who understood she had his best interests at heart. Not the jealous, angry man who came to the church social, or the cold man who'd called on her a few days prior to that.

If he loved her the way she loved him, he would have declared it, especially upon seeing Mr. Emerson do so. But he didn't. Instead, he'd been so rude she couldn't piece him together with the man she thought she'd known.

Molly sat up again, a question forming in her mind. What if he *couldn't* voice his feelings?

It was hard to believe. After all, the man confronted outlaws and general ne'er-do-wells on a daily basis. How could he be upfront with a man bent on causing trouble, but not with her?

But as strange as it was, the more she thought about it, the more it seemed to make sense. It certainly explained the change in his actions toward her, although it didn't excuse them.

What if she gave him another chance?

Molly pushed the quilt back and stood. For the sake of her heart, she needed to know. Did he truly distrust her, or had he spoken out of desperation? Did he understand how much his words and actions had hurt her? And most importantly, did he love her? And was that enough to allow him to trust her if they built a life together?

She would find out whether her dream could become real. Or whether she ought to return to looking among the men of Denver for marriage.

IT WAS BARELY EIGHT thirty when Molly left her aunt and uncle's house. The ride to Eli's mother's house didn't take too long, but it felt like hours passed as she sat impatiently in the carriage. When she finally reached Mrs. Jennings's home, a carriage sat out front with a driver waiting, likely to take Mrs. Jennings on some outing.

Molly accepted the driver's assistance to descend from the carriage. She took a few steps and then paused near the stairs that led to the small front porch. A tiny amount of doubt had crept into her mind, preventing her from placing a foot on the first step. What if Eli refused to see her? Or worse, what if he did, and then informed her she was mistaken—that what they'd had was nothing more than a brief amusement that ended the moment he saw that Mr. Emerson was seriously interested in her?

Molly ran her gloved hands over her dress's simple lilac overskirt. If he did say such a thing, at least she'd have her answer. She could grieve what she'd thought she had and then move on to find a man who did truly love her. Although, even as she thought the words, she could almost feel her heart break in response.

Well, standing here and pondering the maybes would do her no good at all. She lifted her head and forced her feet up the steps. One by one, until she'd reached the door. She lifted one shaking hand to knock. But before her knuckles could touch the wood, a hand clamped over her arm.

Panic rising in her throat, she jerked around to find a man standing behind her.

Eli.

Chapter Twenty-two

MOLLY'S EYES WIDENED when she saw him. Eli drew a finger to his lips when she opened her mouth to speak. She clamped her mouth shut, but raised an eyebrow in question. He held up a finger to indicate he'd explain later and pulled gently on her arm to get her to follow him. What she was doing here, he didn't know. And he didn't dare hope it was because she was thinking about him as much as he'd been thinking about her.

Eli led the way between his mother's house and the one next door to arrive in the rear of the home. He stopped near the back garden, where Mrs. Gowan grew various herbs and vegetables. Glancing at the house before he spoke, he determined they were most likely in the parlor with no way to overhear what he might say to Molly. But he spoke in a low tone just in case.

"I believe the carriage waiting out front is the same one that was here the last time Ma's debt collector paid a visit." He didn't know for certain. After all, black Broughams were everywhere in this town. But it was far too early for visitors, and he'd just happened to go out early for a stroll. When he'd returned and saw the carriage, he *knew*. When Molly's drew up behind it, he'd picked up speed to reach her before she could interrupt the man's conversation with his mother.

Molly's lips formed an "o." "Who is it? Do you know?"

Eli paused a moment, his gaze flicking back to the house before landing on her again. She was so beautiful, he could hardly breathe. She was the kind of girl artists in Europe painted, all raven-haired and fair-skinned. He wanted so badly to run a finger down her cheek, caress her jaw, and draw her toward him. But instead, he needed to tell her that the man inside was most likely her Mr. Emerson, or someone who worked for him. "There is no easy way to tell you this, but I'm fairly certain George Emerson is behind these visits."

Her entire countenance fell, as if he'd gravely disappointed her. "Eli, I came here thinking—"

The back door opened just at that moment, drawing their attention away from each other. Mrs. Gowan stood on the back porch, motioning to Eli.

He wasted no time and moved toward her, Molly on his heels.

"I'm glad you're back so quickly, Mr. Jennings," Mrs. Gowan said. "That man—the one who comes for the money—he's in the parlor with your ma. I came back to the kitchen to start breakfast and saw you out the window."

Eli turned to Molly. "I want you to remain out here with Mrs. Gowan."

Her face turned pink as she glared at him. "I'll do no such thing. If it is Mr. Emerson—which I highly doubt—I have every right to see what he's doing."

Arguing with Molly would be like arguing with a stone wall. Besides, the man wouldn't be intending to stay long. He needed to get in there and catch him in the act of defrauding his mother. "Fine. But I don't want you in the parlor. Keep to the hallway, both of you, and if he gets agitated, I want you out of the house immediately."

Molly nodded her assent, while Mrs. Gowan stated she'd remain safe in the kitchen instead. Silently, Eli pressed the door open and slipped inside with Molly. As they crept down the hallway, voices carried from the parlor.

"This is all I have," Ma was saying. The desperation in her tone ate at Eli's soul. How anyone could torment a widow like this, he didn't understand. The man, Emerson or not, was utterly despicable.

"You promised fifty a month. Surely you have more stashed away. Something from your late husband's estate, perhaps?" Eli paused just outside the parlor door. He didn't recognize the voice, but then he hadn't heard Emerson speak frequently enough to recognize him sight unseen.

"I don't, Mr. Smith, I'm sorry."

Eli peered around the doorframe, his arm holding Molly back. Ma stood facing him, wringing her hands. The man's back was to him, and all Eli could tell was that he wore a black coat and gray trousers, and that he hadn't bothered to remove his hat.

"Oh, look! My son is home. Perhaps you can speak with him and work this out." Ma gestured to Eli, relief evident on her face.

The man jerked around. It took only a second for Eli to recognize him. And when he did, he almost couldn't believe it.

Chapter Twenty-three

MOLLY CLAPPED A HAND over her mouth to keep from gasping. Mr. Carter stood there in the parlor, plain as day, looking guiltily at Eli right after demanding his mother pay fifty dollars a month. Molly didn't think he'd seen her, at least. She'd moved back immediately after he'd turned around.

And now she stood there, glued like paper to the wall in Mrs. Jennings's hallway, trying to breathe normally through her fingers. Mr. Carter! She couldn't believe it.

"What is this about?" Eli asked from just around the corner. "I hear my father owed you debts, and you've been visiting my mother to collect?"

Molly pressed a hand to the doorframe and peeked around it. She could just barely see Mr. Carter over Eli's shoulder. His eyes darted between Eli and Mrs. Jennings.

"Yes, sir," he finally said, taking his hat into his hands. "That's correct."

"How much did my father owe?"

"Approximately two thousand dollars."

Molly's heart nearly stopped.

"Two thousand?" Eli said in a stunned voice. "Whatever did he purchase from a fruit company that cost so much?"

"I'm sorry to say it wasn't a purchase." Mr. Carter's voice was breathy. He seemed nervous. Molly dug her fingers into the wood. Something was strange about all of this. Perhaps it was just as Eli had suspected—Mr. Jennings had owed nothing, and this was a ruse to get money from poor Mrs. Jennings.

"Then what was it? Especially considering the amount increased since the first time you met with my mother." Eli was speaking through gritted teeth. Molly didn't have to see his face to know that.

Mr. Carter didn't reply right away. Instead, he glanced at Mrs. Jennings again, and when his gaze returned to Eli, he wore a pained expression on his face. "It was a series of loans. To keep his business afloat."

"Nonsense. I've been through his accounts. The company was solvent, and was doing quite well before his death."

Mr. Carter shrugged, as if that didn't concern him. "Perhaps it wasn't for the company. I didn't ask. After all, people borrow money for all sorts of reasons. Gambling debts, to repay less savory folks, to—pardon me, ma'am—keep certain women in comfort."

Eli's back was as stiff as the wall Molly stood against, and his hands curled into fists at his sides. Molly couldn't blame him. After all, Mr. Carter just about slandered his father. She only prayed he wouldn't strike out at Mr. Carter.

"I am a man of the law, Carter," Eli said in an even, barely contained tone. "Else you might find yourself in a great deal of pain right now for what you just implied about my father, and in front of his wife, too."

Mr. Carter raised both his hands, as if to ward off any punches Eli might throw at him. "Now, don't get upset. I didn't mean to imply any of that was true. I was merely offering examples. Mr. Jennings borrowed from me—more than once—and I need the debts repaid, that's all."

"There are no debts." Eli took a step toward Mr. Carter.

Molly wanted to reach out and grab his arm, to hold him back and ask him to get the police instead. But she remained where she was, gripping the doorframe for all it was worth while Mrs. Gowan drifted in from the kitchen behind her.

Carter slid to the right, closer to the door as Eli approached him. "I can assure you there were."

"You have no proof." Eli took another step forward, to the side this time, as if he was attempting to keep Carter in the room.

Carter said nothing, but he sidestepped Eli and paused just by the parlor door, mere steps away from Molly.

Mrs. Gowan reached for Molly's hand, indicating they should retreat to the kitchen. The last thing Molly wanted to do now was disappear, not when Eli had Mr. Carter cornered like the coward he was. But she took a step backward with Mrs. Gowan to put distance between them and Mr. Carter.

The movement drew Mr. Carter's attention away from Eli. His blue-gray eyes widened in surprise when he saw her standing in the Jennings's hallway. "Miss Hill! Why are you . . ." He trailed off as he glanced between her and Eli, and his expression hardened as he seemed to come to some sort of conclusion in his mind. "You are quite the opportunist," he said to Eli.

"Don't change the subject," Eli almost growled at Mr. Carter.

Mrs. Jennings drifted back into Molly's view, coming up alongside her son. "Eli . . ."

"Why don't we take a ride over to the city police and sort this out?" Eli said to Mr. Carter, stepping in front of his mother.

The man shifted, and Molly could feel the nervousness wafting off him in waves. Eli's gaze flicked to her, and he jerked his head just slightly toward the kitchen, which sat at the end of the hall.

Mrs. Gowan immediately moved backward, and she tugged at Molly's hand. Molly took a step back, but she refused to hide. If Mr. Carter did something, she wanted to know immediately so she could go for assistance. She was much faster than either Mrs. Jennings or Mrs. Gowan, and besides, her carriage sat waiting just out front. Her heart pounded, but she stayed put even as Eli glared at her. She wouldn't leave him alone in this, whether he loved her or not.

"There's no need to involve the police," Mr. Carter said, his hands going to his hips. Eli's right hand drifted over the pistol that sat holstered, but he didn't remove it. And when Mr. Carter settled his hands on his hips, Eli dropped his hand to his side again.

Molly swallowed as she pressed a hand against the staircase beside her. Surely Mr. Carter wasn't armed. He was hardly the sort of man to carry a weapon. Surely—

Everything happened so quickly that Molly didn't have time to react. Seemingly out of nowhere, Mr. Carter drew a small revolver, and just as Eli drew in response, Mr. Carter had taken three steps to the side and clamped a hand around Molly's arm.

She gasped and tried to pull away as her heart threatened to burst from her chest, but he held fast.

"Leave her out of this." Eli's words were heated. He moved forward, down the hall, both hands grasping the pistol he pointed at Mr. Carter.

"Back away, *Deputy*," Mr. Carter said as he drew Molly in front of him.

She tried to pull away from him, the blood pounding in her ears, but he held firm. Out of the corner of her eye, she could see his revolver pointed at Eli. "Let me go," she spat at him as she tried again to pry his hand off her arm.

Mr. Carter said nothing to her, instead wrenching her arm in front of her as he pulled her against him. If he thought that might keep her still, he was sorely mistaken. Molly pushed against his arm, which was clenched to her stomach.

"Be still," he whispered in her ear, his breath making her shudder. "Lest I shoot your favorite suitor."

Molly froze. He wouldn't. He couldn't, not with Eli aiming at him, too. Unless he was that desperate... Molly couldn't tell, but she wasn't about to put Eli in more danger than he already was.

"We'll be leaving now," Mr. Carter said to Eli, as if this were a pleasant social visit.

"You're going nowhere," Eli said. His voice was even, and the revolver he held on Mr. Carter didn't so much as shake. His entire demeanor was the opposite of how Molly felt at that moment—terrified, jumpy, and wishing for nothing more than the ability to hide in the kitchen as Eli had wanted her to. But even as the thought crossed her mind, she knew she wouldn't have, even if she'd known what would happen. She never would have left Eli to face this alone.

"On the contrary, Miss Hill and I will be leaving in the carriage out front. And you'll be remaining here. I bid you good day, Mr. Jennings." Mr. Carter pressed her forward, and Molly's legs moved reluctantly toward the door.

Eli remained in front of them, revolver on Mr. Carter, refusing to move until Mr. Carter drew the muzzle of his own pistol away from Eli and instead, pointed it toward Molly.

She swallowed hard, seeing the polished metal out of the corner of her eye. Eli's eyes darkened with anger, and he clenched his jaw. He didn't lower his weapon, but stepped backward, out of the hallway and just into the parlor.

"Farther," Mr. Carter said, and after a brief moment during which Molly thought that if Eli could have downed Mr. Carter with only his eyes, he would have, Eli took another few steps back into the parlor, his mother just behind him.

Mrs. Jennings clasped her hands together, her face lined in worry as Mr. Carter nudged Molly sideways down the hallway. Just past the staircase, Mrs. Gowan clutched the kitchen doorframe. No one said a word as they approached the door.

"Open it, Miss Hill, if you please," Mr. Carter said.

Molly choked back a sob. They were leaving and there was nothing she could do to stop it. There was nothing Eli could do. What was going to happen? What would Mr. Carter do with her once they were in the carriage? Where would he take her?

"Now, please." Mr. Carter ground the words out through his teeth, shaking the revolver ever so slightly.

Molly gripped the doorknob awkwardly, given the angle at which he held her, and turned. The door opened inward, and in one quick motion, Mr. Carter led her around the door and sideways down the steps. They walked backward to the carriage, Eli at the door now.

The driver, seemingly unfazed at this turn of events, opened the door while Molly's own driver watched in alarm. Mr. Carter stepped inside, and then pulled Molly in after him. The driver shut the door, and Molly was alone in the carriage with a desperate man.

Chapter Twenty-four

THE SECOND THE BROUGHAM lurched forward, Eli shoved the revolver into its holster and raced down the porch steps past Molly's idling carriage. Carter's driver moved the horse along quickly. Eli pushed himself to run faster through the muck of the street, realizing far too late that he should have taken Molly's carriage. His lungs burned and a few folks out for a morning walk stared at him. Eli barely noticed them. Molly was in that carriage, alone with Carter, and Eli refused to let him get away with her.

He was catching up as the buggy reached the street corner. It would need to slow if it intended to turn—and Eli prayed it would turn. He didn't know what Carter intended to do with Molly once he reached his destination, and he didn't want to find out.

The Brougham arrived at the corner, and to Eli's relief, the driver slowed the horse. That was all he needed. He pushed himself harder and drew even with the carriage on what he thought would be Carter's side. He reached for the door, just out of sight of the window. Just as the carriage began to turn, Eli grasped the handle and yanked the door open.

The carriage swayed and he stumbled backward into the mud. A larger coach swerved around him, but Eli barely noticed. The Brougham came to a halt as the driver jerked around to see what had caused his conveyance to rock sideways.

Carter's face appeared in the doorway. Eli scrambled up, unable to see Molly in the dark interior of the carriage.

"Go!" Carter shouted at the driver as he fumbled with something in his hands.

Eli took no chances, rolling to his side as he approached the buggy and just narrowly missing the shot Carter fired. He gripped the wheel and stood.

"What are you waiting for? Drive!" Carter yelled again. But the driver had leapt to the ground and was backing away toward the confectionery that sat on the corner.

Eli took advantage of Carter's distraction. He reached inside the door and grabbed hold of the man's coat, yanking him out of the Brougham and into the street.

Carter fell ungracefully into the road, his hat landing top down in the mud. Eli was only vaguely aware that horses and carriages around them had come to a halt. Carter recovered quickly, raising the hand that still held the revolver—but Eli moved faster. He leapt from where he stood by the door and grabbed hold of Carter's arm, pushing it back down into the muddy road. The force knocked the revolver from Carter's grasp. Eli kicked at it, sending it further out of the man's reach.

"Mr. Emerson!"

Eli couldn't comprehend why Molly would be calling Emerson's name in the middle of this, but he couldn't think about it for long. Carter was stronger than he looked. The man had grabbed hold of Eli's arm, and with one forceful push, knocked Eli to the side. Eli rose just in time to see Carter crawling to his revolver. Eli reached for his own weapon, but before he could draw, a hand scooped up Carter's gun.

"Hold it right there, Carter," a voice said.

Eli scrambled to his feet, pistol in hand, to see Emerson standing just before them, aiming Carter's small revolver at its owner. Eli stood there, breathing hard and utterly dumbfounded.

Molly appeared at Eli's side in an instant. "Are you hurt?"

He glanced down to find her looking up at him, one hand clutching his arm and the other reaching to turn his face so she could examine it. "I'm fine," he said, still trying to figure out where Emerson had come from. "How are you? Did that coward hurt you?"

"No, I'm fine. But more than ready to see him in jail." She smiled weakly at him. "Thank you for coming after me."

"Pardon me, Jennings, but what did you want to do with this . . ." Emerson trailed off as he eyed Carter, and Eli could only guess at the colorful word he might have used if Molly weren't within earshot.

"Put him in his carriage. We'll take him to the police station."

They got a sputtering, muddy Carter into the Brougham. Emerson found the driver and convinced him to climb back onto the carriage.

"I'm happy to escort Miss Hill home," Emerson said as Eli kept an eye on Carter.

I'm certain you are. Eli looked to Molly. It was the last thing he wanted, but he refused to give in to the jealousy that had consumed him before. Nothing Emerson could say in the next few hours would change Eli's feelings. He'd still apologize for his actions and tell Molly how he felt, as terrifying as it was, and let her decide.

Molly glanced at Eli and gave him a small smile. It was a tiny thing, but it lifted his spirits. Something about it gave him hope.

"Thank you, Mr. Emerson. Might we check on Eli's mother first? I'd like to let her know we're all safe."

"Of course," Emerson replied, though he didn't look thrilled with the idea. Eli nodded his thanks to Molly while his heart swelled with her thoughtfulness.

"Thank you for happening by at just the right time," Molly said to Emerson.

"Well, it was a lucky coincidence." Emerson straightened his tie with a furtive look at Eli.

Eli tried not to smirk. Emerson had been coming to see him. Why, he didn't know, but he was certain it had something to do with their meeting last night. Whether he'd been coming to apologize or demand an apology himself, it didn't matter now. He wasn't the guilty party, and, Eli supposed, he ought to ask Emerson's pardon for his actions last evening.

"I appreciate your help," he said, shifting the pistol to his left hand to extend his right to Emerson.

Emerson paused, then took his outstretched hand. "Glad to provide it."

"My apologies for last evening," Eli added.

Molly knitted her eyebrows as she glanced between them, but to Eli's relief, she said nothing.

"Accepted." Emerson extended his arm to Molly. "And may the best man win."

Indeed, Eli thought as Emerson led Molly away. Just as he slid into the carriage next to Carter, she glanced back at him with a reassuring smile.

"Let's go," he said to the driver. The sooner he delivered Carter, the sooner he could speak with Molly.

Chapter Twenty-five

MOLLY SAT HUDDLED UNDER three quilts, with her feet propped up, and a china cup of steaming tea beside her when Eli arrived later that afternoon.

He stood in the doorway, Stevens hovering next to him, and gave her the most befuddled look.

"Miss Hill, may I present Mr. Jennings?" the butler said in his usual formal manner.

"Thank you," Molly said, and after agreeing to let him inform the kitchen staff that Eli would also enjoy tea and perhaps some cake, Stevens finally left.

"Are you ill?" Eli asked as he entered the room. He sat in one of the wing chairs across from her.

"No." Molly shrugged off the quilts and laid them to the side of her on the settee. "Aunt Ellen has been fussing over me all day. Her remedy for a distressful morning is, apparently, to treat it as if I've caught cold." She breathed deeply as her skin began to cool. Sitting under several quilts in early summer was not the most comfortable experience.

Eli's forehead wrinkled in concern. "I'm sorry about what happened. I should have suspected Carter. Moreover, I should have insisted you remain outside. What happened to you is entirely my fault."

MOLLY 131

"No, the only person at fault is Mr. Carter himself. Did he give an explanation?"

"He didn't. But I assume his fruit company isn't doing as well as he boasted."

"Thank you, again. For everything." Molly sat forward and laid a hand on Eli's arm. It was a natural reaction, and one she didn't think twice about until she'd done it. And now she wasn't certain whether to leave it there or take it back. If she left it, and Eli told her she was mistaken about his interest in her . . . She drew her hand away and looked down at her lap as her cheeks warmed.

"Molly, I . . ."

She swallowed hard and drew her eyes up. Rosa, one of her aunt's kitchen help, had arrived with a tray of tea and little cakes. Eli watched Molly intently as Rosa set the tray down and asked if they needed anything else.

"No. Thank you, Rosa," Molly said, her voice wavering just a little. The girl nodded and left the room.

Eli rubbed his palms on the legs of his trousers as Molly stood and poured him some tea to busy herself. There was a heavy feeling in the air. She'd never felt so awkward around Eli before.

"Sugar or milk?" she asked.

"Sugar," Eli replied.

When she turned to bring him the cup and saucer, he was standing just behind her. She swallowed again and handed him the tea. "Would you like—"

"I'd like to talk to you before I lose the courage," he said, setting the tea back on the tray. "Please."

Molly nodded mutely and clasped her hands together. She didn't dare hope he'd say what she wanted to hear, and yet her heart fluttered traitorously in her chest.

"I've wanted to tell you this for months." Eli's face looked slightly green as he spoke, and his fingers appeared to shake before he shoved them into his pockets.

"Go on," she said softly.

He closed his eyes a moment and drew a deep breath as if he were about to relay an enormous secret. His Adam's apple bobbed, and he gave a wry laugh as he opened his eyes again.

Molly bit her lip. Perhaps it was as she thought, then—that he was terrified to confess his feelings. That fluttering hope grew into a butterfly, beating inside her chest.

He looked toward the parlor door, as if that would give him the courage he needed. Finally, he turned back to her, his eyes a dark green with flecks of brown, and a smile playing across his lips. "Perhaps if I imagine you an outlaw with a shotgun pointed at me, this will be easier."

Laughter bubbled up inside Molly, and she smiled. "Would you like to sit?"

"No. No, standing is better." He looked down at her hands as if debating, and then finally reached for one. His warm fingers curled around hers, and Molly felt as if she'd come home.

"I've admired you for a long time," he finally said, looking at their intertwined hands. "And yet each time I wanted to tell you, courage failed me. Molly, you don't know how happy I was to find you on that train to Denver." He looked up at her, sending a shiver of giddiness down her spine. "And then how I felt as I saw you with Preston and Emerson and every other man who seemed to fall all over himself to be with you."

"I have an idea," she said, remembering what he'd said to her at the church social.

Eli winced. "I am very sorry for how I acted. I let jealousy get the better of me, and I hate that it hurt you. Please know that whatever you decide, I'll accept it. I will not act that way again."

It was exactly what she had hoped to hear. "All right," Molly said, giving him an encouraging smile. "I'll hold you to that promise."

That seemed to buoy him, and he straightened his shoulders. "I'm not a wealthy man. I don't own a company, and I have no need of fancy dinner parties or fine clothing. But Molly Hill—" He raised his other hand and rested it against her cheek, just barely touching her skin. "I love you. With everything I am and everything I have, I love you. I don't know if that's enough, but I pray it is."

A surge of affection flooded Molly from head to toe. She wanted to grab hold of his shoulders and pull him to her and show him how she felt. But she restrained herself with just a smile. His hand grew warmer against her face as she pressed her cheek into his palm. "I thought you'd changed your mind about me. You acted so differently."

"I will never change my mind about you." His thumb grazed the corner of her lips, and she wanted to close her eyes and lose herself in his touch.

"I came all the way to Denver to find someone who saw me as more than Jasper's little sister."

His thumb stilled. "I understand if you'd prefer the sort of life someone like Emerson could give you." His words were strained, and Molly could tell it took everything he had to speak them.

She lifted her free hand and pressed it against his. "I spoke with Mr. Emerson this morning and Mr. Preston earlier this afternoon. Aunt Ellen thought I'd lost my mind, requesting a caller after what happened this morning. I informed them both that as kind as they are, I'm no longer interested in their suit."

Eli stared at her a moment before a smile lifted the corners of his lips. "Might I ask what that means?"

"I believe it means I'm interested in someone else."

He said nothing, as if he were waiting for her to mention some other man she might be infatuated with.

"You," she said. "I love *you*, Eli Jennings."

Any hesitation he felt disappeared from his expression. He pulled her closer until she was flush against him before letting go of her hand to rest his palm against the other side of her face. Sheer joy radiated from his smile, and Molly thought it might be impossible to be happier than she was now.

Well, unless he kissed her, that was.

He lowered his head, his eyes darting across her face as if he wanted to take in every inch of her expression. Molly's eyes closed as his lips met hers, softly at first. Her head seemed to spin as his kiss grew more urgent. It was as if he was finally releasing months of feelings into this one kiss. Molly gripped his arm to steady herself, and when he finally pulled away, she could hardly breathe.

"Is it always like that?" she said, her breath coming in wisps as he dropped his hands to her waist.

"I believe it might be." A wicked grin crossed his face. "Want to find out?"

This time, Molly didn't wait. She stood on her tiptoes to meet him. The world could fall to pieces around them, and she doubted she'd notice. Everything seemed to stop when she was in Eli's arms. And as he deepened the kiss, Molly had one more thought before she lost herself entirely.

If she hadn't come to Denver, she never would have found what she'd had all this time at home.

Epilogue

"HE DOESN'T GIVE ME a moment's rest." Grace eyed the sweet baby boy who was lying comfortably in Molly's arms. "I think I could sleep for a month and I'd still awaken tired."

"I can't imagine this precious baby keeping you up at night," Molly said. He was comfortably warm and heavy in her arms. She ran a soft finger over the wisps of dark hair that lay against his head. He'd have his father's hair, but his bright blue eyes were reminiscent of his mother.

"Imagine it," Jasper said, as he and Eli entered the front door along with a gust of winter wind. "Sam only sleeps in fits and starts."

Molly drew her gaze away from the bundle in her arms to look at her husband and brother. They'd gone to escort Mrs. Hill and Mrs. Jennings home after Christmas dinner. Molly smiled, thinking of the two ladies sharing the home where she and Jasper had grown up. It hadn't taken much convincing on Eli's part to persuade his mother to move with them to Cañon City. And then it had been Molly's mother's idea to ask Mrs. Jennings to stay in her home, now that it would be empty of her grown children. The two ladies were now thick as thieves, and Molly never knew what to expect from them next. This past fall, after Molly and Eli's wedding, it had been raising funds to purchase primers for the town's school. And just today, they'd

MOLLY

announced plans to gather women to knit blankets for the needy babies in Denver. Molly was certain the latter idea had come with little Sam's birth at the beginning of the month.

She wondered what they'd plot when she made her own announcement.

Molly glanced up at Eli as he hung his coat on one of the pegs by the door. His face was red from the cold, but his smile was bright. He made her joyously happy every day, and she'd thought she could want for nothing else—until she'd visited Doctor Bradenton yesterday.

Eli sat in the chair next to hers as Jasper settled next to his wife on the settee. "I don't believe this little fellow is that much of a nuisance. He was quite happy while we ate."

Jasper and Grace shared a knowing smile. "That's because it wasn't the middle of the night," Jasper said. "This baby keeps the hours of an owl."

"Would you like to hold him?" Molly asked Eli.

"I'm not—"

She didn't give him the chance to finish, instead laying the sleeping baby in his arms. Eli held the child awkwardly, as if he were afraid he'd break the baby.

Molly bit her lip to keep from laughing. "You can sit back with him."

Eli slowly relaxed into his chair. Baby Sam raised a tiny fist above his head, and Eli stroked the baby's little fingers with his thumb. His face softened as he looked at his nephew, and Molly thought her heart might melt.

"We ought to get another slice of pie," Grace whispered to Jasper. "Before they give him back."

Jasper didn't hesitate. He stood, clasped Grace's hand, and the two of them darted back to the kitchen in Molly and Eli's little house.

"He is something amazing, isn't he?" Eli said, his eyes still on the baby.

"He is." Molly clasped her hands together. She was more than ready to give him the gift she'd been most excited about. "How might you feel if you were holding one of your own?"

His gaze jerked up from baby Sam to her. He blinked, as if he were trying to understand what she said. "I'd think there isn't anything I might want more."

An enormous smile overtook Molly's face.

"Molly?" he said. "Is there a secret you've been keeping from me?"

She covered her mouth with a hand. Now that she could tell him, she didn't know how to put the wonderful news into words. Eli shifted the baby in his arms and reached over, taking her hand in his.

"It isn't a secret," she finally said, relishing the feel of his warm fingers pressed against her own. "It's something I learned for certain just yesterday, and I thought it might make a nice Christmas gift." She paused. "What do you think?"

"Well, I'm not sure what it is yet. I could use a new pair of gloves. Or one of those saddles that just arrived at the saddlery would be nice."

"Eli Jennings!" Molly exclaimed in annoyance, even though she couldn't keep from laughing.

He clasped the baby to him as if holding the child was no longer a foreign feeling, and stood, drawing Molly up with him. He wrapped his free arm around her waist and pulled her close to him. "If you're saying what I think you're saying, there is nothing I want more."

She looked up into his eyes and all of the emotion they held. "If Jasper and Grace are right, then plan for many sleepless nights next summer."

Eli grinned before ducking his head and catching her lips for a kiss. Molly laughed and returned his kiss, wrapping her arms around him. Baby Sam complained with grunts and short little cries, and Eli drew back, looking down at the baby.

"I ought to thank Paul Carter," Eli said, handing the baby back to Molly.

She cuddled Sam close to her and rocked him back and forth against her chest. "Why is that?" She hadn't thought much about Mr. Carter, not since a judge in Denver sentenced him to repay Mrs. Jennings, with interest, and several months in jail.

"If it weren't for him, I wouldn't have boarded that train for Denver when I did. I might still be visiting you at the store, wishing you'd notice me."

Molly grinned as the baby made cooing noises. "I ought to be thanking the poor man who came into the store and told me about starting his life anew as a miner."

"The . . . what?" Eli asked. "A miner?"

Molly laughed in response.

"Well, whoever he is, I'm awfully thankful to him too." Eli reached for Molly's hand.

She shifted the baby to one side and let her husband draw her in close again. He kissed her a second time, and just as it had that afternoon in Aunt Ellen's parlor, her mind spun and she could think of nothing at all but Eli.

Well, Eli and their soon-to-be new arrival.

THANK YOU FOR READING! I hope you enjoyed Molly and Eli's story. If you enjoyed the Brides of Fremont County series, you might also like my Gilbert Girls series, which is set in the fictional town of Crest Stone, just south of Cañon City. The first book in the series, _Building Forever,_[1] is about Grace's older sister Emma. And some of your favorite Cañon City residents, including Eli, Sheriff Ben Young, and his wife Penny appear in the third book in the series.

To be alerted about my new books, sign up here: http://bit.ly/catsnewsletter I give subscribers a free download of *Forbidden Forever*, a Gilbert Girls prequel novella. You'll also get sneak peeks at upcoming books, insights into the writer life, discounts and deals, inspirations, and so much more. I'd love to have *you* join the fun!

---

1. http://bit.ly/BuildingForeverbook

More Books by Cat Cahill

Books in *The Gilbert Girls* series
Building Forever[1]
Running From Forever[2]
Wild Forever[3]
Hidden Forever[4]
Forever Christmas[5]
On the Edge of Forever[6]
The Gilbert Girls Book Collection – Books 1-3[7]
Crest Stone Mail-Order Brides Series
A Hopeful Bride[8]
Brides of Fremont County Series
Grace[9]
Molly[10]

---

1. http://bit.ly/BuildingForeverbook

2. http://bit.ly/RunningForeverBook

3. http://bit.ly/WildForeverBook

4. http://bit.ly/HiddenForeverBook

5. http://bit.ly/ForeverChristmasBook

6. http://bit.ly/EdgeofForever

7. http://bit.ly/GilbertGirlsBox

8. https://bit.ly/HopefulBride

9. http://bit.ly/ConfusedColorado

10. https://bit.ly/DejectedDenver

The Proxy Brides Series
[A Bride for Isaac](http://bit.ly/BrideforIsaac)
[A Bride for Andrew](https://bit.ly/BrideforAndrew)
The Blizzard Brides Series
[A Groom for Celia](http://bit.ly/GroomforCelia)
The Matchmaker's Ball Series
[Waltzing with Willa](https://bit.ly/WaltzingwithWilla)

About the Author, Cat Cahill

A SUNSET. SNOW ON THE mountains. A roaring river in the spring. A man and a woman who can't fight the love that pulls them together. The danger and uncertainty of life in the Old West. This is what inspires me to write. I hope you find an escape in my books!

I live with my family, my hound dog, and a few cats in Kentucky. When I'm not writing, I'm losing myself in a good book, planning my next travel adventure, doing a puzzle, attempting to garden, or wrangling my kids.

Made in the USA
Monee, IL
21 January 2022